# No Enemies Here

## From the Tales of Dan Coast

# No Enemies Here

## From the Tales of Dan Coast

By

Rodney Riesel

Published by Island Holiday Publishing
East Greenbush, NY

Special thanks to:

Pamela Guerriere

Kevin Cook


Cover Image by:

www.123rf.com/profile_romrodinka

romrodinka / 123RF Stock Photo


Cover Design by:

Connie Fitsik


To learn about my other books friend me at

https://www.facebook.com/rodneyriesel

For Brenda,
Kayleigh, Ethan
& Peyton

# Chapter One

Dan Coast sat in a metal folding chair in a medium-sized conference room at the Big Pine Methodist Church. Ten to twelve other men and women filled about half of the chairs that had been set up before Dan and the others arrived. The chairs were arranged in three rows of eight, with an aisle running down the center. All of the chairs faced a wooden podium at one end of the room. Three ceiling fans spun on high speed above the small crowd. The walls were white, the ceiling was white, and so was the tiled floor. The room was bright and well lit; far brighter than Dan thought comfortable. Every time he entered the room, he wished he were the type of guy who wore sunglasses indoors. But he wasn't, so he left his Wayfarers folded and hanging over the neck line of his T-shirt.

A man stood at the podium. He had short dark hair, peppered with gray. The man wore white cotton slacks, a black belt, and black slip-on dress shoes with no socks. His tight black T-shirt was tucked tightly into his pants. He was dressed better than most of the others in the room, including Dan. The guy, who had introduced himself to the crowd as Drake, was nearing five years of sobriety and was halfway through his story.

"When the cops busted through the hotel room door," Drake explained, "the prostitute who was with me was on the floor and unresponsive. Lucky for me, the paramedics were able to revive her."

Dan glanced around the room at the faces of the others to see if they caught the part about "lucky for me." A few did cock their heads slightly. *Lucky for me*, Dan thought. *What an asshole*.

When Drake finished his story he returned to his seat.

"Thank you, Drake," said, Hal, the moderator.

"Yeah, thanks, Drake," Dan mumbled quietly. The lady sitting in front of Dan looked back and smiled. Dan looked away.

Hal walked back to the podium. "Would anyone else like to share?" he asked.

Dan cleared his throat. A few people turned their heads. "I'm Rick," Dan announced.

"Hi, Rick," everyone said in unison. They waited for more.

"I, uh … I don't have anything to share."

Hal nodded his head a little. "Thank you, Rick," he said.

Dan could feel his face turn red. He was not good in large groups of people … when he was sober. He glanced up at the clock that hung over the door to his left— 10:45a.m., almost over. Dan had been sober for a little over twelve hours, and had even gone for a run before driving up to Big Pine.

8

There were Alcoholics Anonymous meetings in Key West, but Dan figured the farther away he drove, the less likely he would be to run into someone he knew. This was Dan's forth Monday in a row at the meeting. He had tried a few others, but liked this one the best. During these four weeks he hadn't seen anyone he knew, and he hadn't seen anyone from the group outside of a meeting.

Dan liked Hal; he seemed like a nice guy. Drake was a jerk. Ava, the brunette who always sat in front of Dan, was pretty and friendly. She smiled whenever she turned around. She was forty-five, single, and had two children. Dan often thought he wouldn't mind seeing her outside of the group, but they say that's a bad idea. "They" being those whoever wrote The Big Book—the thick as a brick AA bible. Dan wondered what Ava's children were like.

Hal spoke for another ten minutes and then the group disbanded. Outside, Dan put on his sunglasses and headed for his car. Most of the other people did the same. A few, however, congregated around the entrance door, lit cigarettes, and chatted. Dan climbed into his Porsche, started the engine, and pulled out onto Key Deer Boulevard.

Across the street from the Methodist Church was a shopping center, with a Winn-Dixie, a Bealls department store, a Chinese restaurant, a pizza shop, and a handful of other businesses. What caught Dan's eye was the Bagel Island Sandwich Shoppe. He quickly took a left into the parking lot. He drove up and down each lane until he found a parking space and pulled in.

Once inside, Dan walked up to the counter. "Can I help you?" the young female employee asked, with a big smile.

"Yeah," Dan replied. "Can I get a medium coffee, black, and uh"—Dan scanned the available bagels in baskets on the shelf behind the young blonde—"and an everything bagel, toasted, with butter and cream cheese?"

"Coming right up," she said gleefully.

Dan tossed a twenty next to the cash register. The young girl took it and started to count out the change.

"Keep it," Dan said.

"Thank you."

"Look at the walrus, Mom!" came a young boy's voice from behind Dan. "Look at the walrus, Mom."

Dan glanced over at the little kid sitting at one of the tables with his mother. The boy was on his knees in the white wooden chair facing backwards. The mother was on her cell phone.

"Look at the walrus, Mom!"

"Here you go," said the young girl as she handed Dan his coffee. "The bagel will be right up."

"Thank you," Dan replied.

"Look at the walrus, Mom."

Dan looked over at the boy and his mom again, and then up at the humongous cartoon sea creature overhead.

"Look at the walrus, Mom!" The kid continued to point and try to get his mother's attention.

"Here's your bagel."

Dan took the small white paper bag. "Thank you."

"Look at the walrus, Mom. *Mom, look at the walrus!*"

Dan turned away from the counter and made his way over to the table. "Hey," he said.

The woman on her cell phone looked up at Dan. "Excuse me?"

"Hang up your phone," Dan said.

"What are you talking about?"

The girl behind the counter, and the next two people in line, watched quietly.

Dan grabbed the cell out of the woman's hand. He spoke into it, saying, "She can't talk right now," and tapped the end call icon. "You don't know what 'hang up your phone' means?" Dan placed the cell phone on the table in front of her.

"You've got some nerve, mister. I ought—"

"What you ought to do is stay off your goddamn phone and talk to your kid. He's trying to show you something." Dan pointed at the cartoon sea creature. "Look, Mom," he said, an edge to his voice.

The woman scanned the room and made eye contact with a few of the customers. "Well, I never," she said.

Dan looked down at the little boy. "Ya did at least once, but I can't imagine anyone wanted to do it again."

The woman closed her mouth and remained silent.

"It's not a walrus, kid," Dan said. "It's a manatee."

"A manatee," the boy repeated.

"It's not your fault, little fella," Dan said, mussing the boy's hair. "Your mom was probably on her cell phone the day she was supposed to teach ya that."

On Dan's way out of the store he heard the boy say, "Look at the manatee, Mom!"

"I see it, Timmy. That's really neat," said his mother.

When Dan got back to his car, he reached over the door, and placed the paper coffee cup on the dashboard, and then opened the door and got in. He opened the paper bag, reached in, and pulled out the few napkins the girl had stuffed inside, and laid them across his lap. He pulled out the bagel, unwrapped it, and pulled it apart. Most of the cream cheese stuck to the bottom half. Dan laid the bottom half on his lap and took a big bite out of the top half. He reached for his coffee, peeled off the lid, and carefully took a sip, trying his hardest to avoid burning his tongue.

"Hey!" said someone standing next to the Porsche.

"Jesus Christ!" Dan shouted. He jumped, scalding his lip and spilling coffee down the front of his shirt. The bottom of his bagel slid off his lap and landed in the floor, cream cheese side down. "Shit."

Dan looked up to see who it was he wanted to murder. It was Drake.

Drake pointed at the wet spot on Dan's shirt. "You got a little coffee there," he said.

"What the Christ do you want?" Dan asked. He put the coffee cup back on the dashboard and reached into the floor for the bagel.

"You're Rick, right?" Drake asked.

"Uh, yeah," Dan replied.

Drake extended his hand. "Drake Farentino."

Dan shook the man's hand. "Rick … uh … Hunter," he replied. Dan dropped the entire bagel back into the bag and tossed it into the passenger side floor.

"Sorry about your bagel."

"Don't worry about it."

Drake stood with his hands in his pockets looking around the parking lot. The silence was becoming a little awkward.

"Is there something I can do for you, Drake?" Dan asked.

"I, uh … no. I was just going into the bagel place there. I was thinking about getting a coffee and a muffin or something." Drake continued to scan the surroundings.

"Are you waiting for someone?"

"No."

"Okay then," Dan said, and started his car.

"My name's not really Drake," the man blurted out.

Dan looked back up at him and shut off his engine. He waited for more.

"My name's really Lance."

"Lance Farentino?" Dan asked.

"No. Lance Beacon." The man watched an old green Pontiac as it made its way slowly down the lane toward them. The car turned into a parking spot and two older women got out. They headed toward Winn-Dixie. "I just feel stupid telling everyone in there my real name. Crazy, right, Rick?"

"I figure a few of 'em make up names," Dan assured him.

"Ya think?"

"Sure."

"Maybe."

"Is everything okay, Lance?"

"Yeah. Why wouldn't it be?"

"Because you've barely made eye contact with me the whole time we've spoken, and you keep looking around the parking lot like a Secret Service agent."

"Ha-ha. Secret Service. Good one."

Dan started his car again. "Well, you have a good day, Lance."

"You too, Rick." Lance turned and started walking away from the car.

Dan pointed at the bagel shop. "Bagels are that way, Lance."

Lance spun on his heels. "Yeah, that's right. Thanks. Bagels."

Dan backed out of his parking spot.

Lance gave him a wave and said, "See ya next week, Rick."

Dan nodded and drove away.

# Chapter Two

Dan walked up the steps and through the swinging glass door of Red's Bar and Grill. The floor was cleaner than usual and Dan's flip-flops weren't sticking. The old Wurlitzer was softly playing "Into the Mystic." Dan loved the sound of Van Morrison's voice.

Jocko, the cook, was walking out of the men's room; he nodded to Dan. Dan returned the nod.

"What's up?" Red asked, as Dan neared the bar.

"Not much," Dan replied.

"Having a drink?"

"Yeah."

Red grabbed a rocks glass off the shelf behind him.

Dan climbed aboard his favorite bar stool.

Red filled the glass with ice, added tequila, and then filled the rest of the glass with 7Up. He flipped open the lid of the fruit container, picked up a lime wedge, and dropped it in. "Here ya go, pal," he said, sliding the drink across the bar to his friend. "Hungry?"

"No."

"Have you eaten today?"

Dan shot him a look. "Yes, mother. I had two Pop-Tarts for breakfast.

Red looked over his shoulder at the clock. "How long ago was that?"

Dan flipped Red the bird. "About this long ago," he said.

"I can have Jocko whip you up a fish sandwich and some fries."

"I don't want a fish sandwich and fries."

"Ya gotta eat."

"Ya gotta shut up."

Red threw up his hands. "Okay, okay. Sorry." He turned and grabbed a mug off the back bar and filled it with coffee. He blew into the hot drink and took a sip. "You've been moping around here for weeks. I was talking to your mother yester—"

"My mother! What the Christ were you talking to my mother about?"

"Well, the first time I called her—"

"The *first* time?"

"Yeah. I called and talked to her about a week after Maxine left. She asked me to keep her informed."

"So that's why she keeps calling me."

"She's worried about you."

"She's worried about me because you called her," Dan shot back. "If you hadda kept your mouth shut, she wouldn't know anything about it."

"I worry about you too."

"Oh, that's sweet."

Red stepped back and pushed open the kitchen door. "Jocko!" he shouted. "Whip up a fish sandwich and fries."

"I don't want anything to eat."

"You gotta eat."

"Why did I even stop here?"

"Dan the Man!" came Skip's Jeff Spicolie-sque voice from the door. "How they hangin', broham?"

"For the love of Christ," Dan mumbled. "This day just keeps getting better."

Skip slapped his pal on the back and climbed aboard the stool next to him. Skip let his hand linger on Dan's back and even rubbed it a little, to Dan's unease. "Any word from Maxine?" he asked sympathetically.

"No, Skip. Not a word," Dan replied.

"I feel your pain, bro, being apart from your lady sucks donkey dicks," he added, pulling thoughtfully on his wiry goatee.

"Gee, Skip," Dan deadpanned, "you've got a real way with words."

"Eesh. What's it been, seven weeks?"

"Eight weeks, three days," Red offered.

Dan glanced up at the big-headed man behind the bar. "Glad you're keeping track."

"We need a case to work on," said Skip. "Just to get your mind off that little woman."

"I don't want my mind off that little woman," Dan said. "So why don't you mind your own business?"

"Just trying to help, Danno," said Skip.

Dan felt his cell phone vibrate in his pocket, reached for it, and answered. "What?" he asked angrily.

"Might be a case," Skip whispered to Red.

"Dan?" a voice asked from the other end of the call.

"Yeah."

"It's Mel."

"Christ. What now, Mel?"

Mel was Mel Gormin, a man Dan had met over a year ago during his mandatory stay at the Lower Keys Psychiatric Center, where Maxine Myers worked as a nurse. Mel was a retired police detective from Los Angeles who had a bad mental breakdown years earlier after the murder of his wife and daughter. He moved to Key West with his sister, and was now a full-time patient at the psych center.

"It's Maxine, Dan," Mel explained. "She's missing."

Dan sighed. "She's not missing, Mel."

"Well, she hasn't been into work in a long time."

"Mel, we go through this every week. Don't you remember what I told you last week when you called me? Maxine isn't missing. She took some time off from work to go visit her parents. Do you remember me telling you that?"

"When is she coming back?"

"I don't know, Mel."

"Why didn't you go with her?"

Skip and Red were eavesdropping intently.

"She wanted to go by herself."

"Is she coming back?"

"Yes."

"Are you sure? Because she hasn't called me or anything."

"I know."

"Has she called you?"

"No."

"Maybe you should call her just to make sure she's okay."

"I'll try."

"Can you tell her to call me?"

"Sure. I gotta go, Mel."

"Okay. Have her call me. I really miss her."

Dan hung up the phone.

"How's he doing?" Red asked.

"Not good," Dan replied. "I wish Maxine would give him a call."

"Are you sure she's okay?" Red asked.

"She's fine." Dan slid his glass back across the bar.

"Another one?" Red asked.

"Just 7UP," Dan replied.

# Chapter Three

Dan pulled into the driveway at 632 Beach View Street and shut off his engine. He wished the bottle of tequila he used to keep under his car seat was still there. He finished that bottle three weeks earlier and decided not to replace it.

When Maxine left, it was rough. Dan climbed inside a tequila bottle for a little over two weeks before deciding to stop feeling sorry for himself. When he emerged from his drunken state he decided to check out an AA meeting, just to see if it was for him. He quickly decided it *wasn't* for him, but kept going anyway. He heard from others AA members that he should try to hit a meeting once a day at first. Dan figured rather than start big, he would start small and build up. He also made himself a rule to only have one drink at Red's and two drinks at home per day. He had stuck to the rule all but three days during the last four weeks; on those three days he got completely smashed. In his opinion, he was doing pretty well.

Dan got out of his car and walked up the path to his front steps. He pulled open the screen door and walked across the porch. Stepping over the welcome mat that read THE COASTS, he went inside. Buddy's flannel bed was empty. Dan glanced at the photograph of his deceased wife, Alex that sat on the small wooden table next to Buddy's bed, as he walked through the living room.

The television was on; Dan had forgotten to turn it off when he left. A repeat of *Gunsmoke* was playing—a really old, thirty-minute one with Dennis Weaver as Chester. Dan went into the kitchen and poured himself a cup of cold coffee, placed it in the microwave, and hit one minute. While the coffee was heating up he looked out the back door in the direction of Bev's house. Buddy was sound asleep on her back deck.

"Man's best friend," Dan grumbled, stepping back and letting the door shut.

Dan sat in his recliner and stared at the couch with the palm tree print. Everything in the house reminded him of Maxine. He sipped his coffee. His cell phone vibrated. "Goddammit, Mel," he said, and reached into his pocket for the phone. He glanced at the screen, but didn't recognize the number. He answered it anyway.

"What?" Dan answered.

"Dan Coast?" asked a voice at the other end.

"Yeah."

"Mr. Coast, this is Beauregard McSwain. I'm calli—"

"Beauregard," Dan repeated with a little snort. Dan lived the first forty years of his life in upstate New York and never once met anyone by the name of Beauregard. In the few years he had lived in Florida, however, this was about the third person he had met with that old-fashioned, highfalutin name. Dan couldn't imagine a child named Beauregard on the playground when he was a kid. That kid would have caught his fair share of ribbing. But in the South, the name was perfectly acceptable.

"Excuse me?" said Beauregard.

"Nothing," Dan replied. "Go ahead."

Beauregard cleared his throat. "I'm calling on behalf of Mr. Joseph Pantucco."

"You are, are you?" Dan hadn't heard from Joey Pantucco in months. He kind of hoped he would never hear from him again.

Joey Pantucco, or Joey P, as he was more commonly known, was the brother of Jimmy Pantucco. Dan had killed Jimmy P over a year ago. He shot him and fed him to the sharks. Joey didn't know Dan had killed his brother. As far as Joey knew, Jimmy and Dan had been good friends before Jimmy's disappearance.

"Mr. Pantucco would like you to come up to Miami and meet with him at my office at ten o'clock Wednesday morning. The address is—"

"I'm afraid I can't make it, Beauregard. I have some things going on right now and I really can't get away. Tell Joey thanks anyway."

"The address is 555 North East Fifteenth Street, Suite 4C."

"I'm sorry, Beauregard, I can't make—"

"Did you write that address down, Mr. Coast?"

"You're not hearing me, Beauregard."

"Would you like me to give you that address again?"

"Wow. You don't take no for an answer, do you?"

"I assure you, Mr. Coast, it's not I that won't take no for an answer."

"Well, like I said, Beauregard, tell Joey I'm very sorry, but I can't make it." Dan hung up his cell and tossed it onto the end table next to him. "Beauregard. Shee-it.""

Dan picked up the remote control and turned up the volume on the television. *Gunsmoke* had ended and *The Rifleman* was just beginning. He placed the remote on the table next to his cell phone and reclined the La-Z-Boy. As Dan sipped his coffee, he stared over the brim and across the dining room at the bottle of tequila that sat on the bar. He knew he had two drinks coming, but he liked to save them until at least eight o'clock. He sighed, and his attention went back to Lucas McCain. Some fool had just called him a sodbuster. Big mistake. Ole Luke was sure to carve another notch in his Winchester before this episode was over.

# Chapter Four

Tuesday morning at three-fifteen Dan was startled awake by a low grunt from Buddy. Dan opened his eyes and stared at the slow-spinning ceiling fan above him.

Buddy let out another grunt, followed by a quiet growl. Dan looked over the edge of the bed at the dog.

"What's the matter, pal?" Dan asked.

Buddy continued to growl, then he jumped up and headed for the front door.

Dan rolled over and pulled open the nightstand drawer. He grabbed the 9mm he knew was waiting there. Dressed in only his boxers, he tip-toed to the living room.

Buddy sat on the hardwood floor in front of the door; he was still growling.

"Who's out there?" Dan whispered. He walked to the door and pulled it open. Buddy ran outside, barking as he ran.

Dan walked cautiously down his front steps, around the house and down the driveway. "Buddy!" he called out.

When Dan had walked completely around his house, Buddy was waiting for him on the front steps. Dan relaxed. "What the Christ, dog?" he said. "I can think of at least four times someone has broken into this house and there wasn't a peep outta you. Now you wake me up for no reason." Dan went up the steps and through the already open front door. Once inside, he slammed the door behind him.

Buddy lay down on his flannel bed.

"Let me know if you hear anything else, touch-hole. I'm going back to bed."

Dan placed the weapon back in the drawer and climbed into bed. He noticed the recent call light on his cell was blinking. He checked the caller ID, but didn't recognize the number. The voicemail icon was lit. Dan tapped it and put the phone to his ear. He could hear someone breathing, but they said nothing. Dan started to say hello, and then remembered he was listening to a message. The silence lasted about fifteen seconds, and then the call ended. Dan tossed the cell back onto the nightstand, pulled the covers over his shoulder, and went back to sleep.

# Chapter Five

At eight o'clock that same morning, Dan walked down his front steps. He was dressed in a pair of red gym shorts and a blue sleeveless T-shirt. He wore white ankle socks and a pair of running shoes. He had just purchased sneakers the week before. Dan made his way to the sidewalk and stopped. He stretched his arms overhead.

Edna McGee was just pulling two bags of groceries out of her old green Buick. "Morning, Dan!" she shouted.

Dan nodded.

Old man Stein sat on his front steps smoking a cigar. "Mornin', Coast," he said.

"Yeah," Dan grumbled, and gave a little wave.

Dan turned left and started jogging. When he passed the second house down from his, he noticed Julian Thompson sitting on his bike in his front yard. The boy was off the seat, straddling the bar, with both feet on the ground. Dan nodded as he ran by.

Julian smiled. "Hi, Dan," he said.

Dan blamed Maxine for recently getting to know his neighbors. He had lived there for almost four years before Maxine moved in, and at the time, only knew Bev and Edna McGee. Maxine lived there for less than a year, and Dan now knew half the people on his block.

Dan liked being an introvert. He liked it better when he only knew a few people. He liked having a few drinks with Bev now and then, and he liked doing a few things for Edna around her house in exchange for freshly baked cookies and brownies. Dan remembered his life being perfect before Maxine came along, and now that she was gone, it sucked. He wished she hadn't left, and at the same time, he wished he'd never met her.

At about three miles, Dan was almost back home. His cell rang. He slowed and his jog turned into a walk. He answered the cell. "Hello?"

"Dan?" asked a woman's voice.

"Maxine. What's up?" *What's up*, he repeated in his head. *That was stupid.*

"I was just calling to see how you were doing."

"Um … good. How are you doing?"

"Okay, I guess. It was nice to come home."

"How's your parents?" Dan asked.

"They're both good."

"How long are you staying?"

"I haven't really decided."

"Buddy misses you, and Mel calls me about once a week to report that you're missing."

"I should probably give Mel a call."

"Probably a good idea," Dan agreed. "Red keeps asking about you."

"Tell him I said hi."

"I will."

"How's the drinking? Are you taking care of yourself?"

"Are you worried about me?"

"Yes."

"I've been trying to limit my drinking to three drinks a day."

"That's good."

Dan heard Maxine's mother shout her name in the background.

"I have to go," Maxine said. "I'm helping my mother make jam today."

"Okay," Dan said. "I'll talk to you later."

"Bye."

The call ended and Dan whispered, "I miss you."

When Dan put his phone back in his pocket he realized he was standing in front of old man Stein's place. Stein was just finishing up his cigar. Sitting on the step next to him was a Jack and Coke.

"Care for a drink, Coast?" Stein asked, as he lifted the glass and took a sip.

"Kinda early, ain't it, Stein?" Dan replied.

"Seriously, Coast?" Stein asked with one eyebrow raised. "I've seen you puke in the street before noon a few times since you moved in."

Dan grinned foolishly. "I guess you got me there, but I think I'll pass."

"That little woman of yours come back yet?"

"No. She's still up at her parents'."

"Where might that be?"

"Iowa," Dan replied. "A little town called Hedrick."

"Farm girl?"

"Yeah."

Stein stood up. "Tell her the wife and I asked about her."

"I will."

Stein went inside, and Dan crossed the street headed for his own house. Just as he got to the steps, his cell phone rang again. He grabbed it quick.

"Maxine?" he asked without checking the caller ID.

"No," said a gravelly, Jersey-accented voice. "It's Joey Pantucco."

"Hey, Joey," said Dan.

"Hey yourself, Coast."

"What's up, Joey?"

"I was just calling to make sure you were okay. A little birdie told me your girlfriend dumped you and now you've spent the last few weeks acting like a little bitch."

"Ouch, Joey." Dan walked up his steps and into the house. He went straight to the coffee maker.

"Now get your head out of your ass, put on your big boy panties, and get up here to Miami. I need to talk to you about something."

"Can't you just tell me over the phone?" Dan moaned.

"Are you shittin' me? I don't talk business over the phone."

"You're not gonna whack me, are ya?"

"I would say no even if I was, ya friggin' idiot. Now, do you need that address again? McSwain said you wouldn't write it down."

Dan sighed. "Yeah, give it to me again."

Joey rattled off the address and before he hung up said, "Ten o'clock."

"Can Red com—"

The call ended before Dan could finish his sentence. "I'll take that as a yes."

# Chapter Six

"Wow!" Red said. "Two days in a row."

Dan walked across the floor and jumped on his favorite bar stool.

"A little more pep in your step," said Red.

"Shut up," Dan shot back.

"Booze or soda?" Red asked.

"Booze," Dan replied.

Red grabbed the tequila from the well and started making Dan's drink. "Lunch?"

"Sure."

"Fish sandwich and fries?"

"You know it."

Red slid the tequila, Seven, and lime across the bar to his friend, and then stepped back to the kitchen door. "Jocko!" he shouted. "Fish sandwich and fries."

Dan sipped his drink. "I needed that."

"Ya gonna tell me about it?" Red asked.

"Tell you about what?"

"This sudden change in your mood."

"There's no change in my mood."

"Yeah, okay. So you're gonna make me guess."

"Just drop it." Dan took another small sip of the tequila; he wanted it to last as long as possible.

"Did you hear from Maxine?"

Dan nodded. "Yes."

"Nailed it! First try."

"Congratulations."

"Is she coming home?"

"No."

"Did she say when she *is* coming home?"

"No."

"So, what's she been up to?"

"Making jam."

"Huh. I guess that's a farmer thing."

"I guess."

"Did you tell her I asked about her?"

"Yes."

"Did you tell her Mel keeps calling?"

"Yes."

"Did yo—"

"Do you want to take a ride up to Miami with me tomorrow morning?" Dan interrupted.

Red looked to the ceiling. "Let's see, what's tomorrow? Wednesday. Sure, I can do that. Why are we going?"

"Joey Pantucco called me and said he needs to talk to me about something."

Red stared at Dan for a second; his eyes narrowed. "You don't think he found out you killed his brother, do you?"

"You mean, *we* killed his brother."

"You pulled the trigger. What if he's calling you up to Miami to get whacked?"

"Don't be stupid."

"That's why you want me to go, ya bastard. You don't want to die alone."

"We're not gonna die. He just wants to talk about something and he didn't want to do it over the phone."

"Are you bringing a gun?"

"No."

"I wish I had a bulletproof vest."

"He would probably just shoot you in the head."

"Do they have bulletproof hats?"

"I'm sure they do."

"I used to have an old World War II helmet. I wish I still had it."

"Don't you think you would look a little foolish walking around Miami wearing an old combat helmet?"

"Better to look foolish than be dead."

"Dan!" someone shouted from the door. "I've been looking everywhere for you."

Red looked over Dan's shoulder, and Dan spun around. Standing at the front door was Mel Gormin. He was dressed in blue surgical scrubs.

"Mel. What the Christ are you doing here?" Dan asked with great surprise.

"I escaped," Mel replied proudly.

"Well good for you," said Red.

Dan shot Red a disgusted look and returned his attention to Mel. "How the hell did you escape?"

Mel walked toward the bar as he explained. "Down the stairs, down the hall, and through the laundry room. Just like you showed me."

Dan dropped his head and rubbed his temples. "Just like I showed you," he mumbled, remembering the time he and Mel had escaped the psychiatric center. The only difference was, the last time it wasn't a real escape. Dan had been released, and was bringing Mel home for an approved visit.

"Remember, Dan?" Mel asked. "Remember when we escaped and Red picked us up at the Kmarts?"

"I remember," said Dan. "Did you walk here all the way from the hospital?"

"No," Mel replied. "We thumbed a ride."

"You did, did you?" Red said with a chuckle. "Someone actually stopped and ga—"

"Wait, we?" Dan asked. What do you mean *we*?"

"That's the surprise." Mel waved his arm at the door. "Ta-da!"

Dan and Red watched the door. Nothing happened.

"Ta-da!" Mel shouted, a little louder.

Still nothing.

"Billy!" Mel shouted.

Billy Maple stepped into the doorway; he was also dressed in the same blue scrubs.

"What the Christ?" Dan asked.

Billy Maple was another patient Dan had met during his stay at the psych center. Billy was a pyromaniac who had set at least seventeen fires up and down The Keys before being caught. Billy had also been diagnosed with kleptomania, and was remanded to the Lower Key Psychiatric Center after he was deemed incompetent to stand trial. He was around thirty years old, had dark hair and light skin.

"Long time, no see, Dan," Billy said as he made his way to the bar. He hoisted his five foot five body up onto one of the bars tools and studied the bottles on the back bar. "Let me see. I think I'll have a Rob Roy, my good man."

"Comin' right up," Red replied, and reached for the Scotch.

"No it's not comin' right up," Dan argued.

"Told ya," Mel said to Billy. "He's a real dick about anyone but him drinking."

Red continued to make the drink. "What's one drink gonna hurt."

"Yeah, Danny Boy," Billy said. "What's one drink gonna hurt?"

"How do you know what meds this nut is on?" Dan asked.

"Nut?" Billy asked.

"That's very offensive, Dan," Mel added.

"What if the alcohol mixed with his medication makes him crazier?" Dan asked.

"I'm not crazy," Billy shot back. "You take that back."

Red slid the drink over to Billy. "Here ya go, pal," he said. "It's on me."

"Good thing," Dan said. "Because he has no money."

"I do to have money." Billy pulled a nylon tri-fold wallet from the back pocket of his scrubs. He ripped it open, pulled out a fifty-dollar bill, and tossed it on the bar. "Get all my friends a drink," he said, waving his hand toward Mel and Dan, and then downed the drink in one gulp.

"Thank you, Billy," said Mel. "Can I see your wine list, Red?"

Red looked confused. "Jeez, you're the only one who ever asked to see the wine list." He began searching under the bar.

Dan snatched the wallet from Billy's hands, and pulled the driver's license from the clear plastic sleeve. "Who the hell is Mitch Parkinson?" Dan asked, reading the name on the ID.

"For your information," Billy announced, "Mitch Parkinson is my real name."

"Wow, what a coincidence." said Mel. "You have the exact same name as the guy who just gave us a ride here."

"Probably the same address too," said Dan.

"Here, Mel, I found the wine list," said Red. "pardon all the rat crap on it. I really need to call an exterminator." All heads turned. Embarrassed, Red shrugged his beefy shoulders.

Mel studied the wine list. "I think I'll just have a water," he said. Red turned three pissed shades of red.

Billy pushed the fifty across the bar. "Take it out of here."

"Water's free," Red replied.

"You'll never make any money just giving stuff away like that," said Billy. "Another drink, sir."

"No," Dan said.

"What's two drinks gonna hurt?" asked Billy.

"Can I have some money for the jukebox?" Mel asked.

Dan was wishing the one drink rule wasn't in effect for himself. He pulled his cell from his pocket.

"Who are you calling?" Red asked.

Dan nodded his head toward Mel. "This looney bird's sister." Then he motioned to Billy. "And I gotta get someone from the hospital to come pick up this *other* looney bird."

"Sticks and stones," said Mel, "will break my bones, but words will never hurt me."

"Damn straight," Billy echoed, adding as he got up from his stool: "I need to see a man about a horse."

"Make it quick," Dan demanded, "or I'll break your head."

"Yeah, yeah," Billy responded. He stuffed the stolen wallet into the back pocket of his scrubs.

Dan dialed his phone.

A woman answered.

"Stacey?" Dan asked.

"Yes."

"It's Dan Coast."

"Oh, hi, Dan. How are you?"

"Good. I'm calling about your brother."

"Is everything okay?"

"Yeah. He's here at Red's with me," Dan explained. "He escaped from the hospital this morning."

"Escaped? How?"

"I have no idea. I just wanted you to know he was safe, and with me, in case they call you."

"Ask her if I can stay with you," Mel interrupted.

"Thanks, Dan," Stacey said.

"Let me talk to her!" Mel pleaded.

"Bye, Stacey," said Dan.

"Let me talk to her!"

Dan hung up.

"You dick!" Mel shouted.

"Sticks and stones, Mel. Sticks and stones." Dan dialed again.

"Lower Keys Psychiatric Center," came a woman's voice. "How can I help you?"

"I need to speak with Dr. Richards please," Dan said. "It's a matter of life and death."

"Who may I ask is calling?"

"Uh … Dr. Kelly Brackett," Dan replied.

"Please hold."

A few seconds later, Dr. Richards picked up. "This is Dr. Richards. What can I do for you, Dr. Brackett?"

Dan disguised his voice. "Good afternoon, Dr. Richards. I'm calling from Rampart General Hospital in Los Angeles. I have two paramedics who put you down as a personal reference on their applications."

"Oh, okay. And their names?" Richards asked.

"Johnny Gage and Roy DeSoto."

"Hmm … Gage and DeSoto. The names sound familiar, but I would have to look them up in our files. Would it be okay if I called you back in the morning?"

"That would be fine, Sigmund. Let me give you a number whe—"

"Sigmund!" Richards shouted. "Coast, is this you, you jack ass?"

Dan burst into laughter. "Ha-ha. Got you, Sigmund."

"I'm hanging up."

"No, wait," Dan insisted. "I'm calling because I have two of your escapees here with me."

"Escapees? What are you talking about, Coast? What escapees?"

"You didn't even know they were missing, did ya? It's Billy Maple and Mel Gormin."

"If this is another joke, Coast …"

"Check their rooms. They're here with me."

"Jesus Christ! I'll have someone there in a few minutes."

"Okay, but Mel is going to stay with me for a few days."

Mel grinned big and fist-pumped.

"No, he's not," said Richards.

39

"I still have a few compromising photos of you and a certain nurse that says he is. Besides, I already spoke to his sister about it."

"Dammit. Stacey knows Mel escaped?"

"Yeah, but don't worry about it. I'll tell her not to report you. But you owe me one."

"I owe you one? Coast, you're pushing your lu—"

"Just get someone here to pick up this other nut. Or else."

"They'll be there in a second." Richards hung up.

Dan put his cell away and turned to Mel. "Go in the bathroom and get Billy."

Mel jumped off his stool. "On it, partner," he said, and walked swiftly to the men's room.

"Who is Sigmund?" Red asked.

"He's a doctor at the psych center," Dan responded. "His real name isn't Sigmund. I just called him that because he had long, stupid, hippie hair that reminded me of Sigmund from the old Saturday morning show *Sigmund and the Sea Monsters*."

"I remember that show," Red said, gazing into the past. "Uncle Bill, Mr. French."

"Same kid, different show."

"Right. Johnny Whitaker. Freckle-faced kid with ten pounds of red hair."

"That's the one."

Red sniffed haughtily. "I know my sitcoms."

Mel returned to the bar alone and took his seat.

"Where's Billy?" Dan asked.

"Who?" Mel asked.

"Billy," Dan repeated.

"Billy who?"

"Where the hell is he, Mel?"

"I have no idea what you're talking about, Dan."

Dan jumped off his stool and ran to the restroom. He shoved open the door. "Billy!" he called out.

Mel looked at Red and pointed a thumb at Dan, and then circled his ear with his index finger. "Looks like someone needs to head back to the loony bin."

Red chuckled.

Dan exited the bathroom. "The little bastard climbed out the window."

"Who climbed out the window?" Mel asked.

Dan pointed a stern finger at Mel. "You want me to send you back to the hospital?" he asked.

"Oh, you mean Billy Maple. Yes, he jumped out the window and ran for it. He said, 'The man will never take me alive,' as he ran across the parking lot."

"The scrubs he was wearing are wadded up in the bathroom floor," Dan said. "Did he bring other clothes with him?"

"Nope," Mel replied. "He was in his underwear."

# Chapter Seven

Mel sat in Dan's recliner watching *Roseanne*. The foot rest was up and Mel had his fingers interlocked behind his head. Dan was on his cell phone.

"It's not my fault he took off," Dan argued into his cell. "Who would think anyone would fit through that window? Besides, he escaped from the hospital first, under your watch."

"Well, I've had him for four years and this was his first escape," Dr. Richards argued back. "You only had him for twenty minutes. And I think we both know where they learned their escape method."

"You should have tightened security," Dan shot back.

"I didn't think I had to."

"So then, I've taught you a valuable lesson."

"I have to go, Coast. Give me a call if you see him or hear from him."

Dan hung up his phone and turned to Mel. "Get the hell out of my chair," he ordered.

"Well sor-*ee*," said Mel. "Just let me know if I'm an inconvenience."

"You're an inconvenience."

"Ouch," said Mel, as he climbed from the chair and moved to the sofa. "Nice couch."

"Yeah."

Mel lay down, placed his head on the arm rest, and stretched his long legs. "Comfortable too."

"Get your goddamn feet off the couch," Dan said.

"Wow, this place just isn't the same since Maxine was abducted."

"How many times do I have to tell you, Maxine wasn't abducted! She just went up to visit her parents."

"Yeah, that's just what *they* want you to believe."

"Who's they?"

Mel put a finger to his lips to quiet Dan, and then pointed skyward. "They."

Dan shook his head. "I'm not in the mood for this conversation. I'm going out back to read the newspaper."

"You want me to come with you?"

Dan grabbed the paper off the dining room table. "No."

"You want me to make you a drink?"

"No." Dan let the screen door slam behind him and lumbered down the gravel path to the Adirondack chairs.

Mel was already at the back door. "Are you sure you don't want a drink?" he called out.

43

"What the Christ? Yes, I'm sure."

"You seem like you could use one. I think you're stressed out about Maxine's abduction."

Dan took a seat in one of the chairs. "I'm stressed out because of you."

"Ouch."

"Stop saying ouch. That's my line."

"What the Christ?" Mel said, as he turned and headed back to the living room.

Dan glanced over the top of his paper at his dog on Bev's deck. He let out a whistle. Buddy raised his head and looked at his best friend. After seeing Dan had no food or treats to offer, he dropped his head back to the deck and shut his eyes. "You to?" Dan said.

Halfway through the morning funnies, Dan's cell phone rang. *What now?* "Hello?"

"Rick?" a voice asked.

"I think you have the wrong number," Dan replied.

"This isn't Rick Hunter?"

"Oh yeah, that Rick. Who's this?"

"It's Lance. Lance Beacon."

"Do I know you?"

"From the meetings."

"That's right," Dan recalled. "Drake Farentino. You ruined my breakfast yesterday morning."

"Um … yes. That was me."

"Do you want me to call you Drake, or Lance?" Dan asked.

"Call me Drake. That way you won't slip up and say my real name at one of the meetings."

"I wouldn't want that to happen. So, what can I do for you today, Drake?"

"I need your help with something."

"What kind of something?"

"I'd rather not talk about it over the phone."

"Nobody wants to talk about it over the phone."

"Can we meet somewhere?"

"When?"

"Tomorrow?"

"I'll be out of town all day tomorrow. How about Thursday?"

"Thursday is no good. How about Friday afternoon, around one?"

"Sounds good. Where?"

"You know the Galley Grill on Summerland Key?"

"Yes."

"I'll meet you there at one."

"I'll be counting the days," Dan replied, and hung up.

Dan dropped his cell phone onto the ground next to him, and then picked up the newspaper.

"Mel!" Dan shouted. He waited a few seconds, but there was no answer. "Mel!"

"What?" Mel asked from the back door.

"Can you go ahead and make me that drink?"

"Can you go ahead and make me that drink, *what*?" Mel replied, looking for a please.

"Can you go ahead and make me that drink, or I'll send you back to the nut house."

Mel turned and shook his head. "Dick."

"What was that?"

"I said, coming right up."

"That's what I thought you said."

Mel strolled down the gravel path a few minutes later with a drink in his hand for Dan and another glass filled with water for himself. "Here you go," Mel said, handing Dan his cocktail. Mel took a seat in the chair across from Dan.

"Thank you," Dan said.

"You're welcome," said Mel.

Dan sipped his drink. "I wasn't really gonna send you back to the psych center."

"I know." Mel took a big gulp of his water.

"We do have to run over there and grab your medication though."

"Who's gonna give it to me?"

"I will."

"You?"

"Yeah. Why?"

"Maxine usually gives me my meds."

"Well she's not here. I'm sure I can do it just fine. The instructions are right on the side of the bottle."

"You're not a nurse."

"You don't have to be a nurse to give medication."

"What does PRN mean?"

"I have no idea. What does it mean?"

"It means to take a medication when necessary."

"Okay. So?"

"What does PO mean?"

"I don't know."

"It means to take by mouth. See what I mean? You don't know what you're doing. I'll probably end up with my pills shoved up my butt or something."

"Like that would happen, Mel. Have you ever ended up with you pills in your ass?"

"Why, what did you hear?"

"For the love of Christ, Mel." Dan folded his newspaper and picked up his cell phone. "Come on, let's go."

# Chapter Eight

"Hey," Dan said, shaking Mel's shoulder. "Mel! Wake up."

Mel rolled over and rubbed his eyes. "What's the matter?"

"Nothing. It's time to get up."

"Is it a fire drill?"

"No, Mel. I don't have fire drills. We're driving up to Miami this morning."

Mel threw back the covers and swung his legs over the edge of the bed. He was wearing his pajamas with the Star Wars print. "Oh yeah," he said. "We're going up there to look for Maxine."

"No, Mel we're not going to look for Maxine. She wasn't abducted, she just went home to see her parents."

"That's right. What's for breakfast?"

Dan was headed out of the bedroom. "Strawberry or blueberry Pop-Tarts, your choice."

Mel followed Dan down the hall. "You know I hate Pop-Tarts."

"Since when?"

"Since my whole life."

Dan poured dog food into Buddy's bowl, and filled his water dish.

"You want me to call Buddy?" Mel asked.

"Do you know his number?" Dan joked.

"Buddy has a phone?"

"It was a joke, Mel. Buddy's out back."

"Good one." Mel walked through the kitchen to the back door. "Buddy!" he called out. The black and white Border collie/Lab mix came running. "Breakfast is ready, boy." Buddy ran straight to his bowl.

"Go take a shower, Mel, and get dressed," Dan said.

"I need my meds."

"After breakfast."

"I know. I was just testing you. When is breakfast?"

"We'll pick up Red and grab something on the way."

"Good. So then, no Pop-Tarts?"

Dan filled his mug. "No."

"Good." Mel turned and headed for the bathroom.


\*\*\*\*\*


Dan and Mel drove along Atlantic Boulevard on their way to pick up Red. He had told them to pick him up at the bar. The top was down and the radio was on. Kenny Chesney was singing "Key's in the Conch Shell."

"Can I change the channel?" Mel asked.

"No."

"I don't like this song."

"I didn't ask."

"I listen to EDM now."

"What the Christ is EDM?" Dan asked.

"You know, electronic dance music. Techno."

Dan shot his passenger a look. "Are you insane?"

"No. I was tested for that."

"That music is horrible. It's like having a bee stuck inside your head that plays a bass drum."

"How could a bee get inside your head?"

"I think there's one in *your* head."

"So yes, or no, can I change the channel?"

Dan pulled the Porsche into Red's parking lot and parked right in front of the entrance door. "Sure, go ahead."

Just as Mel started switching the channel, Dan shut off the engine. The radio shut off as well.

"Hey," Mel said.

"What? I let you change the channel. What more do you want."

"I wanted to listen to EDM."

Dan opened his door to climb out. "Not gonna happen. Come on."

"The two men walked through the front door. "Hey Red," Mel said.

"Hey, guys," Red responded. "What's up?"

"I got a bee stuck in my head," Mel replied.

"Happens to the best of us, pal," Red said. He walked over to the kitchen door and pushed it open a crack. "Jocko, I'm taking off. Cindy will be in in an hour."

"Roger that," Jocko shot back.

Red started toward the door, and Mel and Dan spun around. Red slapped Mel on the back. "So, is it a bumble bee, or a honey bee?"

"Dan, which is it?" Mel asked.

"It's a son of a bee," Dan replied.

# Chapter Nine

Dan took a left onto North Bayshore Drive and into the parking garage.

"Let's park on the top floor," Mel said.

"We'll park in the first spot we come to," Dan replied.

"I want to park on the top."

"Me too," said Red.

For once Dan did as he was asked, and drove to the top floor and parked. There was only one other car on the roof.

Mel jumped out of the car and stretched. "This is awesome," he said, and ran to the edge of the garage and looked down at the street seven floors below. He then ran to the south-east corner of the garage. "Look, I can see the ocean."

"You've seen the ocean a million times," Dan said. "Come on, we're late."

Mel turned and followed Dan and Red across the roof and to the door beneath the exit sign. "I never saw the ocean from *this* parking garage."

"It's the same ocean," said Dan.

"It's the same ocean," Mel mocked.

"What was that?"

"Nothing."

The three men exited the parking garage, crossed North Bayshore Drive, and entered the building at 555 Northeast 15th Street. They scanned the business directory, and then rode the elevator up to the tenth floor.

"I love elevators," Mel said, as the trio stepped off the elevator and into the lobby of the McSwain and Cardiff Law Firm. "This one time I was trying to rescue some people being held hostage in the Nakatomi Plaza and—"

"That was Bruce Willis in *Die Hard*, not you." Dan pointed at a gray leather sofa in the waiting area. "Go sit over there, Mel" he said. "Red can you wait with him?"

"Well, it was one heck of a Christmas party," Mel recalled.

"Oh, now I'm the babysitter," Red complained.

"I'm not a baby," said Mel. "You're a baby."

Dan turned back to the receptionist and grinned.

"You're a baby," Red shot back.

"Can I help you?" asked the receptionist.

"No one can help me," said Dan.

The receptionist cocked her head.

"I'm Dan Coast. I have a ten-thirty appointment with Beauregard."

The receptionist eyeballed Red and Mel as they quietly argued back and forth over who was the biggest baby. "Please have a seat with your friends, and I'll tell Mr. McSwain that you're here."

"Friends," Dan grumbled. He turned and walked to the waiting area. "Can you two knock it off?"

"He said I was a baby," said Mel.

"Yeah, I don't care," Dan replied. "Just shut up."

About ten excruciating minutes passed before the receptionist said, "Mr. McSwain will see you now."

Dan stood and turned to Mel. "Red's coming in there with me," he explained. "I want you to just sit here. Don't move. Don't talk to anyone. Don't touch anything. Ya got it?"

"What was the second one?" Mel asked.

"Don't talk to anyone," Red answered proudly.

"Very good," said Dan. "Come on."

Red stood, and together the two men walked across the lobby and through a frosted glass door with Beauregard McSwain's name on it. Dan pulled the door open and peeked inside, half expecting to see the floor covered with a plastic tarp to keep his brains from staining the plush navy-blue carpeting.

"Come in Mr. Coast," said McSwain.

"Beauregard?" Dan asked, stepping inside the large corner office with a view of the marina.

"You can call me Beau."

"Okay," Dan said.

To the right of McSwain's desk, sitting on a much nicer leather sofa than the one in the waiting area, was Joey Pantucco. To Joey's right, stood a tall, muscular man in his late twenties or early thirties. The young man had dark hair, slicked back to his scalp. He had dark skin and even darker eyes. It was obvious to Dan that this man and Joey were related.

Joey was dressed in a light gray pinstripe suit, pretty much the same way he was dressed all three times Dan had met with him. The younger kid was dressed in a red nylon track suit, and white sneakers. He stood with his feet a little too far apart and his python arms folded in front of his chest.

Red stayed near the door; Dan walked into the middle of the room.

"I feel like I'm auditioning for *The Sopranos*," Dan said with a stupid grin.

"They canceled that show years ago," the kid shot back.

"And yet, here we are."

Joey laughed. "Dan, this is my nephew on my mother's side, Tony Bianchi. Tony, Dan Coast."

Dan nodded in Tony's direction. Tony ignored the introduction.

Dan turned to his partner. "You remember Red."

"Of course," Joey said. "Tony, you should see this fuckin' guy eat. I had lunch with these two once and Red cleaned his plate, ate what Coast and I didn't, then wanted dessert. He's like a goddamn Olympic eater or somethin'"

Tony's expression didn't change. Not too many things impressed Tony.

"Have a seat guys," Joey said, waving his hand at the two chairs in front of McSwain's desk.

Dan grabbed the back of one of the wooden chairs and turned it slightly to keep McSwain and Joey in view. Red took the other seat.

Joey scooted forward on the sofa and rested his elbows on his knees. "Dan, the reason I asked you up here, is because my nephew, Ricky—Tony's brother—has gone missing."

Dan glanced at Tony for an expression; there was none. *Either he doesn't care that his brother is missing, or his father was a Vulcan*, Dan thought.

"How long has Ricky been missing?" Red asked.

"He disappeared between noon and one Sunday afternoon," Joey replied.

"From where?" Dan asked.

Joey looked to Tony.

"The Wounded Parrot, on Duvall," Tony answered.

"He by himself at the time?" Dan asked.

"He was with Tony," Joey replied.

"Why were you there?" Dan asked.

"We were having a drink," said Tony.

"But, *why* were you there?" Dan asked again.

Tony and Joey glanced at each other, but didn't answer.

"Tony and Ricky were delivering a package," said McSwain.

"For who?" Red asked.

"You don't need to know that," McSwain replied.

"What was in the package?" asked Dan.

McSwain looked to Joey. Joey nodded his head.

"Money," McSwain said.

"How much?" Dan asked.

"That's not important," McSwain responded.

"We'll just say a lot," Dan surmised.

"A whole lot," Joey corrected. "They were supposed to deliver the package, and come right back. No stopping before, no stopping after. There and back, I told them."

Dan stared at Tony for a few seconds and then asked Joey, "Who do you like the best?"

No one answered; they all just looked at each other.

"Who do you like best?" Dan asked again.

"Who do I like best?" Joey repeated. "What do you mean?"

"Ricky or Tony," Dan replied. "Of the two brothers, who is your favorite?"

"I don't have a favorite."

"Everyone has a favorite."

Dan looked at Tony. "Who does he like better?"

Tony tried to laugh it off. "I don't know."

"You know," Dan said. "Is it you, or is it Ricky?"

Tony didn't answer.

"I think he likes Ricky better," Dan decided. "I think he has always liked Ricky better."

"Fuck you," said Tony.

"Was it your idea to go to the bar?" Dan asked.

For the first time Tony unfolded his huge arms and took a menacing step forward. "What are you trying to say, asshole?"

Joey remained silent. His eyes were going back and forth from Dan to Tony.

"I'm not trying to say anything. Your uncle asked me up here to help find your brother. Now I'm doing what he asked me. Was it your idea?"

"No, it was Ricky's."

"Did he speak to anyone … besides you?"

"No."

"Did you?"

"No."

"How many drinks did you have?"

"One each."

"Did you tell anyone you were going to be there?"

"No. I don't talk about that stuff with anyone."

"Would Ricky?"

Tony glanced over at Joey before he spoke. "The kid's got a big mouth sometimes," Tony admitted.

"Why did you look at your uncle? Has Ricky's big mouth been discussed before?"

Tony shook his head. "No."

"I think it has," said Dan. "I think Ricky fucks up a lot and—"

"Watch it, Coast," Joey said calmly. "Tread lightly."

"You never fuck up, do you, Tony?" Dan said. "And it drives you crazy that Ricky's the favorite."

"You son of a bitch!" Tony shouted, and lunged at Dan. Dan tried to get out of the chair in time, but Tony was on top of him.

Red took two quick steps forward, grabbed Tony by the back of his jacket with both hand, and yanked him off of Dan. The big man threw Tony across the room, and took a fighting stance.

Dan rolled to his knees and jumped to his feet.

McSwain remained expressionless in his chair. He acted as if fights in his office were a daily occurrence.

Joey stood. "Knock it off!" he hollered.

Everyone froze.

"I didn't have anything to do with this, Uncle Joey," Tony said. "I swear to God. I don't know what happened to him. He was talkin' to that broad and when I come outta the bathroom he was gone."

"Calm down," Joey said.

"I thought you said he didn't talk to anyone," said Dan.

"There was a blonde chick at the bar. She asked Ricky something. I don't know what she asked him. He laughed. They only talked for a little bit."

"And you went to the bathroom," Dan said.

"Yeah."

"How many times did you go to the bathroom?"

"Twice."

"One drink, and you went twice?"

Tony looked at Joey again. "I had about four drinks," he said defeated.

"And how many did Ricky have?" Dan asked.

Tony took a breath and sighed. "Eight to ten."

"How long were you there?" Joey asked.

"About three hours."

Joey dropped his head and stared at the floor. "You lyin' bastard."

"I'm sorry, Uncle Joey," Tony said.

Joey put up his hand and started for the door. "I'll deal with you later," he said. "Coast, find my nephew, please. McSwain, give Coast that photograph of Ricky." Joey walked out of the office and slammed the door.

Dan looked from Tony to Red, and then to McSwain.

"You heard him," said McSwain. "Find that kid … and the money."

# Chapter Ten

"Can we go to the beach?" Mel asked.

"No," Dan replied.

The three men were crossing the street and headed back to the parking garage.

"I want to go to the beach," Mel insisted.

"No," Dan repeated.

"I sat on that couch the whole time and never got up. I didn't talk to anyone. I didn't look at anyone. I did just what you told me."

"Good for you."

"So I should get to go to the beach."

"That wasn't the deal."

"It should have been the deal."

"You should have mentioned it."

Mel looked over his shoulder at Red. "Can we please go to the beach?" he whispered.

"I'm hungry," said Red.

"Of course you are," Dan replied.

"We should drive over to the beach and grab something to eat."

"Sounds like a good idea to me," Mel agreed.

"Two against one," Red pointed out. He pulled his cell phone from his pocket and began searching for restaurants in the area.

"Fine," Dan said. "We'll go to beach and get something to eat."

"Score!" Mel said.

They climbed into Dan's car and drove around and around to the bottom of the garage and exited onto North Bayshore Drive.

"Which way?" Dan asked.

"Take a left," Red replied.

Dan did as he was told. He drove the Porsche along Venetian Way. Driving over bridge after bridge they crossed Biscayne Island, San Marco Island, and four others before arriving in Miami Beach. He veered left onto Dade Boulevard, and then hung a right onto Twenty-Third Street.

"Where is this place?" Dan asked.

"Turn right up here onto Collins Avenue," said Red.

"Right?"

"Left."

Dan turned left.

"Right there, right there!" Mel said, pointing feverishly at the first empty parking space they came to.

"I see it," Dan said. He whipped a U-turn and pulled into the spot.

The three amigos jumped out of the car and headed for the boardwalk.

"There's a place right up here called the Old Surfer's Tiki Lounge," Red said, as he stared at his Google Maps.

Mel turned down an access path and headed for the beach.

"Wait!" Dan shouted. "Where do you think you're going?"

Mel halted in the sand and turned back. "I'm going to the beach," he replied, as he removed his flip-flops.

"I thought you wanted to eat."

"Order me something. I'll be right back."

"What do you want to drink?"

"Ask to see their wine list." Mel turned and ran toward the water.

When Dan turned back to Red, he was already walking between the two giant tikis that stood at the entrance of The Old Surfer's Tiki Lounge. Dan jogged the twenty yards to catch up.

The Tiki Lounge was an indoor/outdoor beachfront bar. The west side of the big horseshoe-shaped bar sat inside the building and the east side sat outside. The exterior tables and chairs sat in the sand; each table had a LandShark Lager umbrella shading it from the sun. Palm trees lined the perimeter of the dining area and each one was wrapped in a string of white lights. Overhead lights ran from tree to tree above the umbrellas. Ukulele music was coming from hidden speakers.

Red pulled a chair away from one of the four tops and took a seat. "Nice place," he commented.

Dan sat across from Red and craned his neck to keep an eye on Mel, who was now floating on his back in the water. "Look at him."

Red looked at their friend as he splashed in the water. "Not a care in the world."

"Not anymore," Dan said. "I don't know what's better, keeping your mind and remembering every bad thing that happened, or having a breakdown and hiding the bad shit away in some part of your brain where you can't find it."

"I think I would rather keep my wits," Red decided.

"Maybe."

"His wife was murdered, right?" Red asked.

"Yeah, and his little girl. His sister brought him down here after his breakdown. She thought it might help to get him as far away from LA as possible."

"LA, that's where he was a cop?"

"Yeah, a detective."

"And it was two cops he worked with who killed his family?"

"Yeah."

"Maybe forgetting would be better," Red finally agreed.

Dan just nodded his head as he stared out over the boardwalk at his friend frolicking in the sand.

Red stretched his neck in search of a waitress. "I am so thirsty," he commented.

"Yeah, me too," said Dan.

Finally, a redhead in her mid-twenties approached their table. Hre hair was pulled back into a ponytail. She wore white shorts and a blue Hawaiian shirt, unbuttoned and tied in a knot above her belly button. Under the shirt she wore a white sports bra. On her feet were blue deck shoes.

"Sorry for the wait," the waitress said. "My name is Mandy and I'll be your server." Mandy placed a menu in front of each of them. "Can I start you off with something to drink?"

"I'll have a whiskey and ginger ale," Red responded.

"And I'll just have a Coke," said Dan. "And can I also have a glass of water? We have one more joining us."

Mandy jotted down their order and turned toward the bar. "I'll get those right out."

"Also," Dan added, "can I see a wine list?"

"Sure," Mandy said.

"Why does he always ask to see a wine list?" Red asked.

Dan shrugged. "Why does he think a tin foil hat protects him from satellite transmissions? Who the hell knows?"

Mandy returned moments later with the drinks and set them on the table. She handed Dan a wine list that was printed on a thin laminated card. "Are you ready to order?" she asked.

Red stared at the menu. "I'll have a double bacon cheeseburger and a large fry."

"I'll have a fish sandwich with a small fry," Dan said. He glanced out at the beach. "Where the hell did he go? The other guy will have a cheeseburger and a small fry."

Mandy went back inside.

"Do you see him anywhere?" Dan asked. His eyes swept the beach for Mel.

"I don't see him," Red replied.

"Dammit." Dan stood and scanned the crowd. "There he is. What the hell is he doing?"

Mel was standing in the sand with a small white dog under his left arm. He was surrounded by three other men. The men were shirtless, and all wore colorful board shorts.

"I'd better go see what's going on," Dan said.

"Want me to come with you?" Red asked.

"No," Dan replied, "but if you hear me scream, come running."

Red chuckled. "You got it, pal."

Dan took a sip of his Coke and set it back on the table. "I'll be right back." He hurried through the tikis and onto the boardwalk, trying his best to keep Mel in view.

When Dan stepped onto the sand he could see two of the guys were holding beer cans. The third guy stepped toward Mel and reached for the dog. Mel retreated a couple steps. One of the guys laughed.

The guy without a beer reached for the dog again and Mel slapped his hand away.

*Shit*, Dan thought. *This don't look good.* The guy looked pissed, but the other guy kept laughing. Dan finally reached the group. One guy was standing in front of Mel, a second was to that man's left, and the one who seemed to think it was all so funny stood to Mel's right, slightly behind him.

"Hey, guys," Dan said, trying to sound friendly. "What's going on?"

"We're minding our own business," said Beerless Guy. "How about you?"

"Everything alright, Mel?" Dan asked.

Laughing Guy motioned to Mel. "You're girlfriend has my buddy's dog," he said.

"I'm not his girlfriend," Mel shot back.

"Mel, give the gentlemen their dog back," said Dan.

"They were being mean to the dog, Dan," Mel replied. "They were making him drink beer. Dogs can't drink beer. He's going to get sick."

Beerless Guy stepped toward Mel again. "I'm not going to tell you again; give me my dog."

Mel turned to keep himself between the dog and its owner.

"Listen guys," said Dan. "He'll give you the dog back, but ya gotta promise not to let it drink any more beer."

"I'm not giving the dog back," Mel said.

"I'm not promising anything, old man. It's my dog. He'll drink and smoke what I say."

"Dogs can't smoke," said Mel.

The small dog was looking from one person to another as each spoke. The Westie seemed quite content with Mel's arm wrapped around his waist.

"Listen, guys …" Dan said.

As the dog's owner again reached for the Westie, Mel smacked his hand away. The guy doubled his fist and cocked his arm. He swung and Mel ducked.

Mel came up with a right to the man's jaw. Down he went and lay motionless in the sand. Mel brought back his elbow in the same swift motion, smashing Laughing Guy in the nose.

Laughing Guy dropped to his knees with his hands over his face. Blood streamed from his nose.

Mel brought up his foot, kicking the last guy in the nuts. He fell to his knees, and then Mel hit him with a right to the side of the head.

The entire exchange took no more than three seconds. Two men were unconscious in the sand, and the third was sitting on his butt, moaning and holding his nose. The dog didn't seem to care that his master had just had his ass kicked

"Holy shit, Mel," said Dan. "What the Christ?"

"I'm hungry," Mel said. "Did you ask to see the wine list?"

Dan heard a lifeguard's whistle. He looked down the beach to see the lifeguard standing in his chair and pointing in their direction.

"Shit," said Dan. "Drop that dog, Mel ... and run." Dan turned and started running for the boardwalk. "Red!" he hollered.

"My flip-flops!" Mel shouted, as he ran to catch up with Dan.

"Forget the flip-flops."

When Dan rounded the corner onto the boardwalk, he saw two cops on bicycles, about a hundred yards away, riding toward them.

Mel was right behind Dan, the small white dog still in his arms.

Red watched with confusion as Dan ran back through the tikis and past their table.

"Gotta go," Dan said, on his way by.

"What?" Red asked.

Mel hurried past the table. "I got a new dog, Red."

"Huh?" asked Red. He took a sip of his drink, and watched his two friends run through the bar, across the interior dining room floor, and out the front door onto the street.

The two officers pulled up on their bikes, put down the kickstands, and entered the The Tiki Lounge. "Did you see two guys run by here?" one of the officers asked, as the other scanned the dining area, his fists doubled and resting on his hips.

"Was one of them carrying a dog?" Red asked.

"Yeah, that's them," said the other officer.

"They didn't come in here," Red informed the cops. He pointed down the boardwalk in the opposite direction. "They ran past me and down that way."

"Thanks," said the first cop. The men in blue returned to their bikes, and continued on down the boardwalk.

Mandy returned with a tray containing the three lunches. "Mandy," Red said. "I hate to do this to you, but I'm gonna need those to go, please."

# Chapter Eleven

"You owe me seventy-three dollars," Red said.

"Seventy-three dollars?" Dan repeated. "It was a couple burgers."

"It was three lunches, two drinks, and a tip," Red argued.

Dan drove the Porsche south along the Overseas Highway through Tavernier. Red was in the passenger seat, and Mel was sitting in the backseat … talking to his new dog.

"You're going to love Key West," Mel told the Westie.

"You can't keep the dog," Dan informed him.

"Don't you listen to him," Mel said. "He hasn't been drinking much, and it makes him a real dick sometimes."

Red laughed out loud. "You got that right," he said.

"Richards ain't gonna let you keep a dog at the nut house," Dan said.

"I'll just tell him he's my service dog," said Mel. "Then he has to let me keep him."

"I don't think it works that way," Dan said.

"I think it does," argued Red.

"Doesn't he have to be registered or something?" asked Dan.

"Who, the dog or Mel?" Red replied.

"Ha-ha, the dog."

"Who's gonna check?"

"All I know is that I'm not gonna get stuck with another goddamn dog," Dan said.

"What should I name him?" Mel asked.

"Are ya sure it's a him?" Dan asked.

Mel lifted the dog and checked its undercarriage. "Positive."

"How about Sandy?" Red suggested. "You got him at the beach."

"How about Felony," Dan offered. "Because you stole him and kicked the shit out of three guys."

"I didn't steal him," Mel shot back. "I rescued him."

"Yeah," Dan agreed. "The same way bank robbers rescue money from the bank."

"I think I'll name him Boozer," Mel decided.

"Boozer?" Red asked.

"He was drinking a lot of beer at the beach," Mel said.

"Good name," said Red.

"How do you like that name, little fella?" Mel asked the dog. The Westie gave a little yip. "Then Boozer it is." Mel hugged the dog tightly.

Dan glanced up in the rearview mirror. "Don't squeeze him too hard, Lenny."

"Okay, George," Mel replied.

# Chapter Twelve

Buddy was already growling before Dan and Mel walked through the front door. Mel was carrying his new dog.

Dan walked past Buddy, who was lying on his flannel bed, next to the table that held a photograph of Alex. "Doesn't sound like Buddy wants to make friends," he commented.

"Sure he does." Mel squatted down and set the dog on the hardwood floor between his feet. "Boozer, this is Buddy. Buddy, this is your new friend Boozer. He's going to be living here for a while."

"No he's not," Dan called out from the kitchen.

"Yes he is," Mel whispered.

Buddy continued to growl at the new house guest. As Mel slid Boozer forward on the slippery floor, Buddy's growl became more menacing.

"I wouldn't do that," Dan said. "Just bring that dog in here and let Buddy get to know him on his own terms."

"Alright," Mel sighed. He picked up the dog and went into the kitchen.

Buddy laid his head back on the bed.

"I need to get him a collar," said Mel.

"You do, do ya?"

"Yeah, and a leash, so I can take him for a walk."

"Is that it?" Dan grabbed a coffee mug out of the cupboard and filled it with cold coffee from the coffee pot.

"He'll probably need a water dish and a food bowl. Do you think he can eat the same food as Buddy, or should we get him some puppy food?"

Dan placed his cup in the microwave and hit one minute. He turned and scratched Boozer's head. "I don't think he's a puppy, Mel. This dog looks like he's at least seven or eight years old."

"How will we know for sure?"

"Cut him in half and count the rings."

"What!"

"I'm kidding, Mel." The microwave dinged. Dan turned and removed his cup.

"We better bring him to a vet for a checkup. Boy, this is really going to cost me."

"Yeah," Dan said. "It'll probably cost *me*."

"I have money," Mel argued.

"I know you do."

"And a Ferrari … just like Magnum's."

"I know, Mel."

"I just have to ask my sister for the money."

"Let's not ask her just yet. I don't want her to know I let you keep the damn dog."

Mel turned and went back to the living room. "I'm going to watch some TV."

"You hungry?"

"No."

"You gotta eat in the next hour so you can take your pills."

"I don't think I need to take the pills anymore." Mel sat down in the recliner and turned on the television. "I think I'm cured."

"Probably," Dan shot back sarcastically, "but we'll keep taking them just to be on the safe side."

"Whatever," said Mel. He placed Boozer on his lap. "You like *Gunsmoke*, little fella?"

Dan's cell phone vibrated in the pocket of his cargo shorts. "Hello?" he answered.

"Rick?"

"Yeah."

"It's Lance … er, I mean, Drake."

"Yeah."

"We still on for Friday at one?"

"Yut."

"Okay. Just making sure."

"Why, is something wrong?"

"No. I'll see you Friday at the Galley Grill."

"Okay."

Drake ended the call, and Dan slipped his cell back into his pocket. *Maybe I should bring some of Mel's medication for Drake*, Dan thought. He shrugged his shoulders and went in to watch *Gunsmoke*.

# Chapter Thirteen

It was morning. Dan sat in one of his Adirondack chairs reading the morning edition of the Key West Citizen. He had a full cup of coffee sitting in the dirt next to his chair and an unfrosted blueberry Pop-Tart resting on his knee. Buddy lay on the ground in front of him. Dan had his feet resting on the mutt's back.

Dan was halfway through a story about a woman who had been run over while crossing Flagler Avenue. The person driving the car left the scene. "People are real assholes, dog," he commented. Buddy ignored him.

"Morning, neighbor," said Bev, Dan's next door neighbor.

Dan lowered his paper and peered over the top at the attractive blonde in her late fifties. "Mornin', Bev," Dan returned. "Have a seat."

Bev had brought with her her own cup of coffee. She sat down in the chair across from Dan. "Where's your houseguest this morning?" she asked.

"Which one?"

"How many you got?"

"Two—a Mel *and* his dog."

"You bought him a dog?"

"No. He stole one at the beach while we were in Miami."

"The more questions I ask, the more confusing the story gets."

"Welcome to my world." Dan folded the newspaper and offered it to Bev. She declined. He tossed it on the ground, and picked up his cup of coffee.

"Any word from Maxine?" Bev asked.

"She called."

"When?"

"Day before yesterday."

"That's good."

"Hmm."

"Isn't it?"

"I guess."

"She say when she's coming back?"

"No."

"How's the drinking going?"

"Trying to stick with the two a day."

"Still going to the meetings?"

"Yup."

"That's good."

"That reminds me," Dan said. "You ever hear of a guy by the name of Lance Beacon?"

Bev shook her head. "Doesn't sound familiar."

"How about Drake Farentino?"

"No. They both sound like characters from a soap opera."

"They're both the same guy."

"What do you mean?"

"This guy, Drake Farentino, he goes to the same AA meetings I go to … on Monday mornings. He started coming the week after I did. After the last meeting, he follows me across the street to this little strip mall and waits for me to come out of the bagel shop. When I get back to my car he comes over and talks for a while. He acted as though our meeting was a coincidence, but I'm sure it wasn't. He seemed really nervous and watched all the cars that entered the mall as we spoke. He barely made eye contact with me the whole time. Then he tells me his real name is Lance Beacon, and that he uses the Farentino alias at the meetings."

"Maybe he's somebody who doesn't want his name associated with AA, or being a drunk," Bev offered.

"Ouch," Dan said. "Maybe. But the thing is, I gave him a fake name too."

Bev chuckled. "Sounds like something you would do."

"Then Tuesday I get a phone call from him. He says he wants to meet with me. Says he needs my help with something."

"You gave him a fake name and never gave him your number."

"Exactly."

"Did you ask him how he got your number?"

"No."

"So, he probably knows who you really are."

"That's what I'm thinking."

"Well, be careful."

"I'm always careful."

"No you're not. That's why you're presently living by yourself."

"Ouch again, and I'm not living by myself. I have a wacky guest from the loony bin, and two friggin dogs."

"I remember when you loved being alone," Bev recalled. "And now you'll do just about anything to have company. You're a changed man, Coast."

"You want me to tell you what you are?"

Bev pointed a finger at her neighbor. "Watch it, pal."

"Beautiful Bev!" Mel shouted from the kitchen door. He was shirtless and in his pajama bottoms. "Long time, no see."

"Well good morning, Mel," Bev replied.

"Let me grab a cup of coffee and I'll be right out."

"No coffee," Dan said. He picked up the Pop-Tart that had been balancing on his knee and took a bite.

"Let me put on a shirt," said Mel. "Wait right there, I've got something to show you."

"Will do," Bev responded.

A few minutes later, Mel walked through the screen door and down the steps carrying his dog. "Look what I've got here," he said.

"Well, what have we here?" Bev said, acting surprised.

"It's a dog, Bev."

"I can see that. Where did you get him?"

"I stole him from some douche bags at the beach."

Bev shot Dan a look. "He's starting to sound like you."

"My protégé," Dan commented.

"What's his name?" Bev asked.

"Boozer."

"Boozer," Bev repeated. "Good name. Does he like booze?"

"No. He likes beer, but he's not supposed to drink it because he's a dog."

Bev scratched the dog between the ears. Buddy watched closely and growled. He didn't like one of his friends petting another dog.

"Quiet, dog," Dan ordered.

Buddy got up and walked slowly across the yard toward Bev's back deck.

"Buddy doesn't seem to like him," Mel commented. "But I'm sure they will be best friends in no time. Just like me and Dan."

"Yeah, just like us," said Dan.

# Chapter Fourteen

Dan and Mel pulled into the parking lot of Red's Bar and Grill around one o'clock. They backed into a parking spot on the far side of the lot and got out of the car.

"I don't know why I couldn't bring him with us." Mel said angrily.

"Because he's a dog, and I've got work to do," Dan replied.

"I would keep him out of the way."

"You can barely keep yourself out of the way."

"Ouch."

Dan stopped in his tracks and pointed at Mel. "Stop saying that."

"Stop saying what?"

"Ouch."

"Why can't I say *ouch*?" Mel kept walking.

"Because it's my line."

"You don't own it."

Dan grabbed Mel by the shoulder and turned him around. "Listen," he said. "Actually, I do own it. I trademarked the word ouch."

Mel stared at his friend. "Really?"

"Yes. It's mine now."

"I don't believe you."

"I have the paperwork at home if you want to see it."

Mel continued to glare at his friend.

"I'm just trying to protect you, Mel," Dan said. "If you keep saying ouch, I could sue you."

"You could?"

"Yes. But I don't want to do that, because we're friends."

Mel smiled. "Thanks, Dan. You're always looking after me."

"What are friends for?" Dan asked.

Mel turned and the two continued across the parking lot.

"Oh, and Mel," Dan said, "let's just keep this ouch business between the two of us."

"Mums the word."

"Also," Dan added, "you can't use the words douche bag, ass bag, or shit bag."

"Wow," Mel sighed. "That's four words I can't use anymore."

The two men walked up the steps and Dan pulled open the door to let Mel enter first. "We'll pick you up a dictionary on the way home. See if you can't come up with some words of your own."

"Thanks, Dan."

Dan's flip-flops stuck to the floor as he walked to his barstool.

"Good afternoon, gentlemen," said Red, from behind the bar. His uniform of the day was cargo shorts with a camouflage print and a red Hawaiian shirt that was unbuttoned just a little too far. "What can I get you?"

"A guy with a mop," Dan replied. "When was the last time you mopped that floor, for chrissakes?"

"Yesterday," Red retorted. "It was busy last night."

"Can I see your wine list?" asked Mel.

"Here ya go," Red responded, tossing the small thin cardboard list in front of Mel. "I cleaned all the rat crap off it."

"Ginger ale," Dan said.

"Water for me," said Mel.

Red made their drinks and then refilled his own cup of coffee. "I take it we're heading over to the Wounded Parrot first," he surmised.

"As good a place to start as any," Dan replied. "You ready to go?"

"Yeah, just a second. I got Jocko whipping me up a sandwich. I haven't eaten all day."

Dan gave a slight grin. "You haven't eaten *all* day?" he questioned.

"No."

"Nothing?"

"No. Why?"

"You had nothing for breakfast?"

"I had one donut, but that was like six o'clock," Red admitted.

"And nothing since then?"

"God, you're a dick."

"How many donuts did you have?"

"Maybe like two."

"And then?"

Jocko walked out of the kitchen with a plate in his hand. On the plate was a turkey club. "Here ya go, Red," he said, sitting the plate on the bar in front of his boss.

"Is that the only thing you made him today, Jocko?" Dan asked.

"Yeah, I think so. That, and breakfast."

"That'll be all, Jock," Red interrupted.

"What did you make him for breakfast?"

Jocko's eyes shot to Red. "What was it, boss, three eggs, bacon, and toast?"

"Yeah, Jocko," Red sighed.

Dan laughed. "Haven't eaten all day," he mocked.

"I hate you," Red said to Dan.

"I know you do, pal. I know you do."

Red picked up the sandwich in both hands and took a huge bite.

Dan watched as his friend chewed with his mouth open. "It's like watching Bigfoot rip into a wild boar."

"Ouch," said Red.

"You can't say that anymore, Red," Mel informed him. "Dan holds the copy—"

"Mums the word," Dan reminded him.

Mel covered his mouth with his hand. "Oops."

# Chapter Fifteen

Dan pulled to the curb on Duval Street, about two blocks down from the Wounded Parrot. As Dan climbed out of the car, his cell phone rang. *What now*?, he thought. "Hello?"

"Coast, it's Joey Pantucco."

"I know."

"Is that my sister?" Mel shouted.

Dan ignored him.

"What have you found out, Coast?" Joey asked.

"I haven't found out anything, Joey. I haven't even started."

"What the hell are you waiting for?"

"It's not even noon."

"Is that my sister?" Mel asked again. "I have to tell her about the dog."

"What did you do last night?" Joey asked.

"Seriously?" Dan gave Red a look as though Red could hear both sides of the conversation. "Are you gonna call me every day to check up on me?"

"Well, yeah, probably. This is very important to me. You have to find my nephew, Coast."

"I know, Joey. I said I would do what I could. Now hang up and let me work."

"Work," Joey repeated with a chuckle. "You crazy bastard, just find that kid."

The call ended and Dan shoved the phone back into his pocket.

"Was that your boss checking up on ya?" Red asked.

"You know it," Dan replied.

Dan stepped up on the sidewalk and the three men headed toward the Wounded Parrot.

"Who was it?" Mel asked.

"Who was what?" Dan replied.

"Who was on the phone?"

"It was your sister." Dan lied.

"Why didn't you let me talk to her?"

"Oh, did you want to speak to her?"

"It wasn't your sister, Mel," said Red. "Ignore him. He's just bustin' your balls."

The Wounded Parrot was a small bar, frequented mostly by locals. The facade of the building was yellow clapboards with green trim. There was a solid pine entrance door stained dark brown. Painted on the door was a giant six-foot parrot on crutches, with one of his wings in a sling. There were also two large picture windows in the front, one on each side of the door.

Red pulled open the big wooden door to allow Dan and Mel to enter first. Dan removed his sunglasses the second he entered the room and tucked them into the neck of his shirt. About half of the eight or nine patrons turned to see the new arrivals, and then returned their attentions to their drinks or their companions.

Red stepped inside and let the door swing shut behind him.

The bar ran the full length of the wall opposite the door. Six round tables, with four chairs at each, scattered the room in no particular order or design. The jukebox against the south wall played Van Morrison's *Moondance*. The interior walls were unfinished rough-cut spruce. The suspended ceiling was 2x2 tiles that, along with the grid work, had long ago been painted black.

Dan made his way through the tables and to the bar, where he climbed aboard a barstool near the middle. Mel sat to his right, and Red took a seat on his left.

A tall, skinny bartender with a shaved head stopped wiping down the bar and slung the bar rag over his shoulder. "What can I get for you gentlemen?" he asked. He cracked his knuckles like he was readying himself for a gunfight.

"Tequila, Seven, and lime," Dan said.

Red surveyed the tap handles. "I'll have a Blue Moon."

"Can I see your wine list, my good man?" asked Mel.

Dan shook his head.

"Wine list?" The bartender seemed stumped. "We got red … and we got white."

Mel put his index finger to his chin. "*Hmm*. I'll have a water."

"Wise ass," the bartender muttered.

Dan slid a hundred-dollar bill across the bar and waited as the young man made their drinks. "Take it out of this," Dan said, tapping the hundred with his middle finger.

"Here ya go," said the bartender, placing the drinks in front of each of them. He snatched up the hundred, turned, placed it in the till, and then counted out Dan's change. The kid pushed the change across the bar, and Dan pushed it back.

"I was wondering if you could answer a few questions for me," Dan said, his index finger still on the bills.

The kid stared at the change. "You a cop?" he asked.

Dan had never been asked that question in his life. A weird kind of pride rose inside him. In that moment he felt just like Magnum or Rockford. He wondered how one of them would respond, and then it came to him. "Do I look like a cop?" Dan wanted so badly to make eye contact with Red, but he knew his friend would be grinning, and Dan wanted to remain serious. Dan reached out his hand. "Dan Coast."

The kid shook. "Albert," he announced.

Mel and Red sipped their drinks.

"Can I play the jukebox?" Mel asked.

Dan and Red ignored him.

"Were you working here last Sunday afternoon, Albert?" Dan asked.

Albert looked to the ceiling as though that's where the answers were kept. "Let's see … Sunday. Yep, I was here."

Dan pulled the photograph of Ricky Bianchi from the side pocket of his cargo shorts and placed it on the bar top.

"This guy came in here with his brother Sunday and they had a few drinks. Do you remember him?"

Albert studied the photo like there would be a test. He nodded his head. "Yeah … yeah. I 'member them guys. This one here in the picture"—Albert pointed at the photograph—"was pretty drunk, kind of a loudmouth. The other one—the older guy—he was quieter, didn't drink as much."

"Did they argue or fight about anything?" Dan asked.

"Can I play the jukebox?" Mel asked.

"What the Christ!" Dan said. "Red, take him over there and let him play the damn jukebox."

Red sighed loudly. "Sure," he said, "the babysitter will do it." He climbed off the barstool. "Come on, Mel."

Albert watched the two cross the room. "That guy daft or somethin'?" he asked.

"Or somethin'" Dan replied. "Where were we?"

"You asked if they argued or fought."

"Did they?"

"No, but the older one did seem to be kinda angry with the younger one."

"Angry, how?"

"He kept sayin', 'Come on, we gotta get goin','"

"Did he mention where they were going?"

"No. The younger one just kept laughin' it off and tellin' that girl that his brother was always tryin' to act like he was the boss."

"Who was the girl?"

"Don't know. Never saw her before in my life. Pretty blonde chick. Little too skinny, but a pretty face."

91

"How old was she?"

"I don't know. I told ya I didn't know her."

"Well how old did she look? Was she my age?"

Albert shook his head. "No, no, not that old. No offense."

"None taken." Dan could hear Mel and Red quietly arguing at the jukebox. He looked over to see Red slap Mel's hand away from the coin slot and say, "No!" Dan returned his attention to Albert.

"She was maybe thirty."

"The older one, Tony, he said he went to the bathroom and when he came out, his brother was gone, and so was the girl. Did his brother leave with the girl?"

"Don't know. I was changin' a keg and when I come out of the back room, the younger one, Ricky, he was gone; so was the girl. His brother asked if I saw where they went. I told him I didn't. He left, and that was the last I seen of either one of them."

Dan looked around the room. "Any security cameras?"

Albert threw a thumb over his shoulder. "Just that one up there that points at the cash register, but it wouldn't show much else."

The jukebox finally started playing; it was William Shatner's "ham on wry" rendition of *"Rocket Man."*

*Good God*, Dan thought. He got off his stool. "Thanks for your help, Albert." He pulled a business card from his pocket and handed it to the bartender. "My name and number are on the card. If you think of anything else that might help, give me a call."

Albert took the card and looked it over. "I'll do that," he said.

Dan picked up the photograph of Ricky and started for the door. He turned back. "What were they all drinking?"

Albert thought for a second. "The younger one was drinking Scotch on the rocks, and his brother was drinking beer—Bud Light, I think."

"And the girl?"

"Diet Coke."

"How long was the girl here before the guys got here?"

Albert shrugged. "Ten minutes?"

"She talk to you?"

"Just to order the pop."

Dan turned back to the door. "Come on, ya morons," he said, making his way through the maze of tables.

"My song just started," Mel complained.

"Yeah, I don't care," Dan said on his way out the door. He pulled his aviators from the neck hole of his shirt and slipped them on. "Come on!"

Heading back to the car, Red asked, "He have anything useful to say?"

"Not really," Dan replied.

"I didn't get to hear my song," Mel complained.

"Do I look like a cop?" Red asked, poking fun at Dan.

"Shut up," said Dan.

"Someone owes me a dollar," Mel demanded.

"It was my dollar," Red reminded him.

The three amigos climbed back into the Porsche and Dan started the engine. He turned to Red in the passenger seat. "I thought that sounded pretty cool," he said.

"What sounded pretty cool?" Red asked.

"When I said, 'Do I look like a cop?'" Dan put the car in drive.

"Yeah," Red said. "I have to give that one to ya. It was pretty cool."

Mel reached forward and patted Dan on the shoulder. "You're the coolest guy I know, Dan."

"Thanks, Mel."

"Isn't there something you want to say to me, Dan?" Mel asked.

"Yeah," Dan admitted. "You're the craziest person *I* know."

"Thanks, Dan," said Mel.

"What are friends for, pal?"

# Chapter Sixteen

The following morning Dan slipped on his running shoes and tied them. He grabbed a T-shirt out of his dresser drawer and put it on. Quietly tiptoeing down the hallway, he gently pushed open the door to Mel's bedroom. Mel was sound asleep; lying next to him on the bed was his best friend, Boozer. The dog lifted his head when he heard the door creak, saw it was Dan, and dropped his head back down on the blanket. Dan pulled the door closed and went out into the living room.

Buddy was lying on his bed. Dan knelt down and scratched the dog between the ears. "Keep an eye on those two," he said. "I'll be back in about twenty minutes."

Dan did some pre-run stretching on the sidewalk in front of his house. He looked up the street one way and down the other. The only sign of life on the whole street was Edna McGee watching him from her front picture window. Dan waved and Edna waved back. She smiled and then let the curtain fall back into place.

Dan ran the same two-mile route he had been running a few mornings a week for the past few weeks: down his street, right onto Ashby Street, left onto Atlantic Boulevard, right at White Street; then right on United, down to George, and home. He walked the full length of his street and back to cool down.

Buddy was still in bed when Dan got back inside; so were Mel and Boozer. He went to the bathroom to splash some cold water on his face and over his head, and then went to the kitchen to make coffee. When he checked his cell phone, there was a message. He tapped the voicemail icon and listened.

"Hey, Coast, it's Joey. Just checking to see how things were going. Give me a call."

"What the Christ?" Dan said under his breath.

There was a knock at the door. Dan turned to see Edna McGee. She had a plate covered with plastic wrap in her hand. Dan waved her in.

"You're up early," Edna said.

Dan's eyes went to the plate full of chocolate chip cookies. "Yeah," he said. "Thought I would go for a run."

"I baked you some cookies." Edna set the plate on the dining room table.

"I see that." Dan reached under the plastic wrap and grabbed a cookie. "I was wondering what I was going to have for breakfast."

"You didn't eat breakfast yet?" Edna started for the kitchen. "How about I whip you up something, dear?"

"No, you don't have to do that."

"It would be my pleasure. Have you been eating properly? You look like you've lost weight."

"Probably from the running." Dan followed her into the kitchen.

Edna opened the refrigerator and pulled out the carton of eggs.

"Really, Edna, you don't have to make me breakfast."

Edna ignored him and opened a cupboard, looking for a frying pan.

"Next door over," Dan informed her.

"How are you doing with the drinking?"

"Um … good." Dan wondered if everyone in town knew about his attempt at semi-sobriety.

"Still going to the meetings?"

"Yeah."

"Scrambled or fried?"

"Scrambled, please."

"I spoke with your mom yesterday. She said you hadn't heard from Maxine."

"She did, did she?"

"Have you?" Edna scrambled three eggs in a bowl and then dumped them into the hot pan.

"Yes. She called Tuesday morning."

"That's great. She say when she's coming home?"

"Nope."

"You should call your mom."

"Apparently I don't need to. Everyone else seems to keep her up to date on things."

Edna placed two pieces of bread into the toaster. "Everyone is worried about you."

"Good morning, Elegant Edna," Mel sang out from the kitchen doorway. "Are you making us breakfast?"

"Yes, I am," Edna replied. "What would you like, Mel?"

"I'll have two eggs over medium with bacon, hash browns, and toast."

"There's no bacon or potatoes, Mel. I can do the eggs and the toast."

"Good enough," said Mel. "Dan, did you bring in the paper?"

"Nope."

"I'll get it," Mel said. "I want to see if they caught the guy who ran over that lady on Flagler Avenue the other day." Mel turned and headed for the front door. "We should take that case, Dan."

"We already got a case, Mel."

"What are you working on?" Edna asked.

"My mother didn't tell you?"

"Smart ass," Edna said. "Go sit down and I'll bring you your plate."

"Yes, ma'am."

# Chapter Seventeen

Dan pulled off of A1A and into the parking lot of the Galley Grill and parked. When he got out of his car he scanned the parking lot. There were seven or eight other cars, but Dan had no idea what Lance Beacon drove.

The Galley Grill was a one-story block building painted pastel green. The name of the place was written in large black letters on the front of the building, up near the roof. There was a covered patio out front surrounded on all sides by wooden lattice.

Dan walked inside the patio and saw Beacon sitting at one of the booths; he was looking at a menu and had a cup of coffee sitting in front of him. When Beacon spotted Dan, he put down the menu and waved him over.

"Hey, Rick," said Beacon. "Thanks for coming."

Dan slid into the booth across from Beacon. "Okay," he said. "First of all, let's cut the shit. You know my name isn't really Rick Hunter or you wouldn't have been able to get my cell phone number."

Beacon looked a little embarrassed. "Yeah," he admitted. "You're Dan Coast."

"I know I am, and you're Lance Beacon. Let's just call each other by our real names from this point on."

Beacon nodded. "Whatever you say." He looked away and summoned the waitress. She hurried over.

"Are you ready to order?" she asked Beacon.

"Yeah. I'm going to have the cheeseburger and fries."

She turned to Dan. "And you, sir?"

"Just the coffee, Thanks."

"Are you sure?" Beacon asked. "The burgers here are really good."

"Just coffee."

The waitress turned and walked inside.

"So, why am I here?" Dan asked.

Beacon sipped his coffee. "It's a long story."

Dan sighed. "Not too long, I hope."

"Well, I—"

"Just start from the beginning."

"Okay. About six weeks ago, I was sitting in a bar—"

"You married, Beacon?"

"Yeah."

"Got kids?"

"Yeah."

"How many?"

"Three."

"What was the name of the bar?"

"Showgirls."

"What's that, like Chuck E Cheese's?"

"No, it's a gentl—"

"Yeah, I figured." The waitress brought Dan's coffee. He thanked her and said to Beacon, "Keep going."

I was sitting at the bar, blitzed out of my mind."

"Afternoon … evening?"

"Four in the afternoon. I stopped after work."

"You do that a lot?"

"Not anymore."

"Go ahead." Dan took a drink of his coffee and then blew in it. The coffee wasn't that hot, it was just a reflex.

"I had a bit of a drinking problem back then."

"And now?"

"I haven't had a drink in three weeks; since the first day I came to one of the meetings."

"That's great," Dan said. Dan didn't give a shit if Beacon was still drinking or not, but figured the positive reinforcement couldn't hurt.

"Thanks. " A car pulled up slowly and parked next to Dan's Porsche. Beacon squinted his eyes to see through the latticework.

"Someone you know?" Dan asked.

"No."

"So, you were sitting in a bar … and?"

"This guy was sitting next to me."

"How old?"

"I don't know. Mid-thirties, maybe."

"Was this guy as drunk as you?"

"He had had a few, but nowhere near as many as me."

"Because you had a bit of a drinking problem back then."

Beacon ignored the jab. "We got to talking … well, I was doing most of the talking. I told him how my wife had taken the kids and went to stay with her mother. I told him about my job, and that I was on unpaid leave because of something that had happened."

"What happened?"

"I came in drunk and passed out at my desk."

Dan grinned. "Ha-ha. They hate that. Where do you work?"

"Cameo Designs. I work in advertising."

"Where is that located?"

"Cutler Bay."

"And you live?"

"Cutler Bay."

"And where is your favorite bar, Showgirls, located?"

"That's also in Cutler Bay."

"Excuse me," Dan said to the waitress on her way past the table. "Can I get a piece of paper and a pen or pencil?"

"Sure," she replied. The young girl went inside and promptly returned with a blank sheet of copy paper and a pen.

"Thanks," Dan said. He began writing down some of the things Beacon had told him.

Beacon waited patiently as he kept his eyes on the parking lot.

"What's your address?" Dan asked.

"19401 Ridgeland Drive. Beautiful five-bedroom overlooking Whispering Pines."

"That a golf course?"

"No, a lake."

"Showgirls?"

"South Dixie Highway."

"Okay, back to the guy sitting next to you."

"I was pretty depressed. I told the guy that I wished I was dead."

"That's understandable."

"The guy turns to me. He gets this look in his eyes."

"Look?"

"Yeah, like he was all of a sudden a different person. He says, 'Well, you're in luck. Making wishes come true is a hobby of mine.'"

"That's scary."

"At the time, I laughed it off. I asked him what he meant by that. He told me he was a contract killer. I asked, 'Like a hitman?' He said, 'Exactly like a hitman.'"

Dan stared at Beacon for a second. "Please tell me you didn't ask that man to kill you."

"I asked that man to kill me."

"You're an idiot."

"I was drunk."

"What did he say next?"

"He said he was leaving the country and had another job to take care of first, but that I would be hearing from him soon."

"Did you pay him?"

"No. He said he would do me pro bono ... because he liked me."

"Well, you gotta admit, that was pretty nice of him. What with you being out of work and all."

"I finally went back to work and my wife came back home."

"Sounds like a country song in reverse. Have you heard from him since?"

"I noticed the same car drive by my house several times, and about two weeks after I spoke with him, someone tried to run me off the road."

"Did you go to the cops?"

"He also mentioned that. He said if I went to the cops, it would be much more painful."

"Ouch."

"Yeah."

"And how long have you been hiding out down here?"

"Three weeks. My wife thinks I'm here on business."

"Did you get the guy's name?"

"No. Coast, you have to help me. This guy knows where I live. I have a family."

The waitress delivered Beacon's burger and set the plate in front of him. "Here you go," she said. "Is there anything else I can get for you?"

"I don't think so," Beacon replied.

"A bulletproof vest," Dan said. "Oh, and a helmet."

"Excuse me?" said the waitress.

"Never mind," Dan said.

Beacon took a big bite of his burger. "You're kind of a smart-ass," he said with a mouthful.

"No one's ever told me that before."

"I bet."

Dan readied his pen. "Where are you staying?"

"At the Big Pine Key Hotel."

"And everything has been fine so far?"

"So far. He must not know where I am. But I'm thinking it's only a matter of time."

"I'll follow you back to your hotel after you finish stuffing that burger in your face and—"

"I'm finished," Beacon said, cramming the last of it into his mouth. He took one last drink of his coffee, got up, and threw a twenty and a five onto the table. "Let's go."

Dan tossed a ten-dollar bill of his own on the table and together the two men exited the diner.

"Beacon," Dan asked, "what about the dead hooker?"

"What dead hooker?"

"The story you told at the AA meeting."

"Oh," Beacon chuckled. "I got that story from a movie I saw once. That never really happened."

"What the Christ is wrong with you?"

"I thought it sounded like a cool story. Besides, I couldn't tell the real story."

Dan pulled out his sunglasses, put them on, and looked up at the cloudless sky above. He wondered how Bev was making out watching Mel and his dog. Then he heard the squalling tires. He turned his head toward the street to see a black Chevy Malibu traveling south and skidding sideways. Dan looked to Beacon, whose eyes were the size of dinner plates.

The ass end of the Chevy slid around and came to a stop, the front of the vehicle now facing north. The window lowered and both men could see the sawed-off double-barreled 12 gauge pointing at them.

"Holy shit!" Beacon cried out.

Dan hit Beacon in the chest with both hands, sending him flying backwards over the hood of a Subaru.

"Stay down!" Dan shouted.

One of the barrels flashed and the Subaru's rear window exploded.

Dan turned and dove into the front seat of his Porsche.

The second barrel fired, hitting the latticework to the left of the doorway and sending small shards of pressure-treated wood into the patio dining area. Dan kept his head down as he fumbled to open his glove box in search of his 9mm. He could hear screams coming from the diners on the patio.

"Coast!" Beacon yelled.

When Dan came up with his weapon the Malibu was spinning its tires down A1A. He pointed the chrome 9mm at the Chevy, wondering if he should take a shot; he decided against it. "See if everyone is okay in there," Dan hollered to Beacon.

Beacon jumped from his hiding spot and ran to the diner. When Dan joined him, they helped several people to their feet.

"Is everyone okay?" Dan asked. It appeared that no one had been injured.

"That was too close," Beacon said.

Dan turned to the parking lot. "Which car is yours?"

"The Subaru with no rear window," Beacon replied.

For a second Dan thought about leaving the scene until he heard the sirens. *Dammit!* he thought.

# Chapter Eighteen

It was dark by the time Dan got back from Summerland Key, by way of the Monroe County Sheriff's Station on Cujoe Key. Dan, along with Lance Beacon, answered all of the questions in the usual Dan Coast fashion. "I've never seen that man before in my life." "I can't imagine why anyone would be shooting at me." "I only know Mr. Beacon from our AA meetings." "Am I free to leave?"

Dan walked up his front steps and through the front door. Lance Beacon followed close behind with a small backpack slung over his shoulder.

"Where am I sleeping?" Beacon asked.

Dan pointed to the other side of the room. "Right there on the couch."

"You don't have a spare bedroom?"

"Yup."

"Can't I sleep in there?"

"Nope."

"Why?"

"It's already taken," Dan replied. "Believe it or not, you're not the only guest at the Dan Coast Bed and Breakfast."

"You married?"

"No."

"Oh. I just saw the doormat that said THE COASTS, so I assumed you were married. Divorced?"

"No. I just couldn't find a mat that read THE COAST."

"Gotcha. Where should I put my backpack?"

"Over there on the floor by your bed," Dan said, waving his arm toward the couch. He continued on through the living room and into the dining room. He walked up to the bar that sat against the wall. "You want a drink?" Dan unscrewed the cap off the tequila.

"I could use one," said Beacon.

"Me too," Dan agreed. "What'll ya have?"

"Whatever you're having is fine."

Dan carried two glasses into the kitchen and filled them with ice, and then returned to bar, where he added tequila and 7Up. "Here ya go," Dan said, handing Beacon his drink.

Beacon downed half the drink in one gulp. "Oh, man," he sighed. "First drink in almost a month."

"Glad I could help."

Beacon walked over and sat on the couch. He put his feet up on the coffee table. "Pretty nice place you have here, Coast," he commented. "What brought you down to the Keys?"

Dan turned and started for the back door. "My car," he said. "I'll be back in a sec. I gotta run next door and grab my other houseguest and his dog. Make yourself at home. The bathroom is down the hall, on the right." With that, Dan was out the door and on his way over to Bev's.

"Hey, you made it," Bev announced, when Dan came through the back door. "Didn't go as planned, huh?"

"Does it ever?" Dan asked.

Mel was sitting on the couch with his bare feet pulled up underneath him. An old rerun of *The Brady Bunch* where Peter broke Marcia's nose with the football was playing on the television. Boozer was curled up next to Mel, but jumped from the couch when he saw Dan enter. He ran to Dan and started humping his leg.

"What the Christ?" Dan said, pushing the dog away.

"He likes you," Mel stated.

"Yeah, but I just want to be friends."

Bev laughed.

"You ready to go, Mel?" Dan asked.

"This is almost over."

"It just started, Mel," said Bev. "If you hurry over to Dan's and put it on there, you won't miss much."

"Good idea." Mel leapt from the couch and ran out the back door.

Dan bent to pick up Mel's flip-flops. "You forgot your—"

The screen door slammed shut.

Boozer ran to the door.

"Thanks, Bev." Dan turned and headed home, grabbing Mel's dog on his way through the door.

When Dan walked into his living room, Mel was sitting in Dan's recliner; *The Brady Bunch* was now on *his* television.

"You forgot your shoes and your dog," Dan said.

"Oh, yeah," said Mel.

"Mel, that's Lance Beacon. Beacon, Mel."

Both men glanced over at one another and said "Hey," then their eyes went back to the Bradys.

Dan's cell phone rang. He looked at the caller ID. It was Joey Pantucco. "For the love of Christ!" Dan said, and slipped the phone back into his pocket without answering it. Then he made his way to the bar for another drink.

The Brady Bunch went to a commercial break and Mel looked over at their new roommate. "Why are you staying with us?"

"It's a long story," Beacon replied.

"Someone's trying to kill him," said Dan.

"Who?" Mel asked.

"He hired a hitman to kill him," Dan responded.

Mel's eyes went to Dan and then back to Beacon. "You hired your own hitman … to kill you?"

Beacon looked a little embarrassed. "Yeah."

"Huh," Mel said. "And they say I'm crazy."

# Chapter Nineteen

Dan had done his best the night before to keep the two-drink-a-night deal he had made with himself. It didn't happen that way, however. He lay in bed the following morning staring at the motionless ceiling fan blades wondering how many he had drunk. *Couldn't have been more than five*, he figured. He turned his head and looked at the clock. 8:38. He had a slight headache and rubbed his temples. He thought about running and quickly pushed that notion out of his head.

He threw back the sheet and swung his legs over the edge of the bed. He got dressed in the same cargo shorts and T-shirt he had worn the day before, and then went to take a leak.

Beacon was still sound asleep on the couch when Dan walked into the living room. He was lying on his side covered with the blanket Maxine kept over the back of the couch, and facing the back of the couch. Dan wondered if *he* would be able to sleep so soundly knowing someone was out there trying to kill *him*.

Dan went to the kitchen to put on the coffee, and then to the front porch to retrieve his morning paper. None of this seemed to stir Beacon. Dan grabbed a package of unfrosted blueberry Pop-Tarts and carried them, along with his paper and coffee, out to the Adirondack chairs. He figured the longer Mel and Beacon slept, the longer he would have peace and quiet.

He placed his coffee cup on the ground next to him and balanced the Pop-Tarts on his knee. That's when his cell phone rang and ended his peace and quiet. The call was from Key West's chief of police, Rick Carver.

"Hello?" Dan grumbled.

"Coast?"

"Yeah."

"It's Rick."

"I know."

"What the hell are you doing now?"

"Eating a Pop-Tart and drinking a cup of coffee."

"You know what I'm talking about."

"Apparently, I don't."

"First I hear you're down at the Wounded Parrot asking a bunch of questions, and this morning I find out you were involved in a shootout up in Summerland Key."

"It wasn't really a shootout," Dan explained. "Someone just fired a shotgun at the front of the Galley Grill. The guy was probably just disappointed with his service. I doubt he was shooting at me."

"They're always shooting at you," Rick argued. "What's the reason this time?"

"I have no idea what you're talking about. I was there having lunch with an old friend. When we walked out of

113

the building, someone emptied a double-barrel into the building … and badly ruined a Subaru."

"Very funny. Who was this friend you were having lunch with?"

"An old friend from high school," Dan lied.

"And where is this friend now?"

"Headed home, I guess."

"Bullshit! What does your friend have to do with the Wounded Parrot?"

"Nothing. That's a whole different thing."

"So, you're admitting there's a thing."

"I gotta go, Rick," said Dan, "I just stepped in some dog shit."

"Coast!"

"Bye." Dan hung up the cell and tossed it into the dirt next to his coffee cup. *Huh*, Dan thought as he skimmed the headlines. *I gotta go. I just stepped in some dog shit. That's pretty good. I'll have to use that again some time.*

Dan made it almost to page three before the back screen door opened and out ran Boozer.

*What the Christ!*

"Morning," said Mel.

"Yeah," Dan replied.

Boozer ran straight for Dan's leg and began making love.

"Go on, dog," Dan ordered, as he tried to shoo the dog away with his foot.

Mel walked down to the Adirondack chairs carrying a large glass of water and a package of Pop-Tarts. He sat across from Dan and ripped open the package with his teeth. He took a large bite out of one of the pastries. "Yum," he said.

"I thought you said you hated Pop-Tarts," Dan recalled.

"What?" Mel asked. "Don't be crazy. I love Pop-Tarts.

Dan bit into his own breakfast treat. "Beacon awake?"

"Nope," Mel replied. He tossed a small corner of the Pop-Tart to Boozer. Boozer snatched it out of the air and swallowed it whole. "Chew it, Boozer."

"Mornin', neighbors," Bev called out from her back deck. She was holding her own mug of coffee and a half eaten English muffin.

"Beautiful Bev!" Mel called out. "Come on over."

Bev reached back and pulled open her door, allowing Buddy to exit. Buddy ran to his master, keeping a close eye on Boozer as he ran. Buddy sniffed Dan's leg and then gave him a look, as if to say, "I know your leg was cheating on me," and then lay down beside the Adirondack chair.

"Get up," Dan said to Mel, "and let Bev sit down."

Mel jumped up and grabbed one of the folding chairs from the shed and placed it next to Bev's chair.

"Read about you in the paper this morning," Bev commented, taking a seat.

"Really?" Dan replied. "I didn't think that would be in there until tomorrow."

"Was I in the paper?" Mel asked.

"What did you do?" Dan asked.

"Nothing."

"Then why would you be in the paper?"

Mel shrugged and tossed his dog another chunk of Pop-Tart. "I don't know."

"What time does the paper usually come?" Dan asked.

"Around five," Bev replied. "Sometimes a little sooner."

"Huh."

"What's up?" Red called out, as he made his way down the driveway and into the backyard.

"Hey, Red!" Mel hollered.

"Mel," Dan said, "get another folding chair for Red."

Mel jumped up, and then paused. "Why do I keep having to get everyone's chair?"

"Because you're the guest." Dan replied. "The guest always gets the chairs."

Mel continued on his way to the shed. "I had no idea."

Red took a seat in Mel's chair. "Does the guest also get me a cup of coffee?" he asked.

Mel unfolded the chair and placed it next to Dan's chair.

"Mel, would you get Red a cup of coffee?" asked Dan.

"Sure," Mel replied.

"And wake Beacon up," Dan added.

"Who's Beacon?" Red asked.

"A guy I'm working for. He stayed here last night."

"Is that his black Malibu out front?" Red asked.

"No. He didn't—holy shit!" Dan jumped to his feet a started running for the house. "Come on, Red. Bev, call 911."

Dan passed Mel on the gravel path; Red was right behind him. He yanked open the screen door and ran into the house.

When Dan and Red got to the living room, Beacon was on the floor. A red headed, freckle-faced guy in his early thirties was stooped over behind Beacon. He was wearing black leather gloves and had a dark nylon cord wrapped around Beacon's neck. Beacon, his face blue, frantically tugged at the cord. His bare feet whipped against the hardwood, squeaking but gaining no traction.

The red head's eyes went to Dan, and then to Red, and then to his sawed-off double-barreled shotgun lying on Dan's coffee table.

Dan lunged for the shotgun at the exact same time as the stranger released his grip on Beacon, and also leapt for the gun.

Dan grabbed the barrel and the red head grabbed the butt. The red head pulled the trigger, firing one of the barrels and blowing a bowling ball-sized hole through the back of the couch.

Both men got to their knees. The weapon fired again, this time into the ceiling, bringing chunks of plaster down on everyone's head.

Red continued to side-step the commotion, planning his move.

Beacon lay on his back, still gasping for air.

The stranger brought the butt of the shotgun up against the side of Dan's head. Dan let go of the barrel and fell backwards. Everything went fuzzy.

The intruder jumped to his feet and pointed the empty weapon at Red.

Red grinned and took a step toward him.

The stranger turned, and running as fast as he could, catapulted himself through the front picture window and onto his back on the lawn.

When Red got to the window, the ginger was already climbing into his car.

Red turned just in time to see Dan's eyes roll back in his head as he toppled over backwards onto his back.

# Chapter Twenty

Dan Coast sat in his living room on one of his dining room chairs. Red was behind him, leaning against the dining room table. Bev had taken Mel and the dogs over to her house.

"Lunch with an old friend from high school, huh?" Rick said. He stood facing Dan with his arms folded and resting on his large belly. His aviators rested on top of his head.

Dan stared at the floor, rubbing a spot just below his temple. "Okay, I lied," he said. "He's a friend from grade school."

Rick placed the palm of his hand on his police issue revolver. "One more lie comes outta your mouth and I'm gonna shoot ya."

Dan threw a thumb over his shoulder at Red. "With a witness standing right there?"

"I'll shoot him too," Rick responded.

"I didn't do anything," Red complained.

119

"I don't care," said Rick. "Now, start from the beginning."

"I was born in a small town in upstate—"

"I'm not in the mood, Coast."

"Alright, alright," Dan said. "Beacon hired a hitman to kill him."

"Suicide by hitman?" Rick asked.

"Yup. His wife had left him, he was about to lose his job, and he was drunk and depressed. He was in a bar and joked to the guy next to him that he wished he was dead. He just happened to be sitting next to a guy who was more than happy to oblige."

"Did he pay him?" Rick asked.

"Nope. The guy said he would do it for free ... 'cause he liked him."

"You know who this guy is?"

"No, but at least now we have a description."

"Yeah," Red chimed in. "He looks like a grown-up Johnny Whitaker."

Rick shot him a thousand-yard stare and turned to Dan.

"Your neighbor across the street, Stein, got a plate number. We ran it. The plates were stolen off another vehicle." Rick looked back at Red. "You been in on this from the beginning?"

"I'm hearing the details for the first time," Red answered. "I've only been helping him with the other thing."

Dan shook his head.

"What other thing?" Rick asked.

"Um …"

"There's no other thing," Dan argued.

"He said, 'other thing.'"

"We were thinking about looking into that thing on Flagler Avenue," said Dan, making up the story as quick as he could.

"Yeah, that thing," Red agreed.

"What thing?" Rick asked.

"That hit and run."

"Why would you be looking into that? Who asked you?"

"Nobody," Dan said.

"Yeah, nobody," Red repeated. "We just felt bad, and thought it would be a nice thing to do."

"Yeah, right," Rick said. "Just don't get in anyone else's way."

"Like who?" Dan asked.

"Like the investigator who's working on the hit and run."

"We won't," Dan said.

"Promise," Red added, drawing a cross over his chest with his index finger.

Dan stood and swayed a little. He steadied himself. "Let's get over to the hospital and check on Beacon."

"Let your idiot friend drive," Rick said, pointing at Red. "You don't need to be driving after a hit on the head like that."

"Roger that," Dan said. "I feel like half my brain is gone."

Rick snorted. "In other words, all of it."

"What about the window?" Red asked.

Dan said, "We'll worry about that later."

The three men started for the door.

"What if someone breaks in?" Red asked. "They could climb right through that window."

Dan turned to his big friend. "Someone did break in, and having a window there didn't stop them at all."

# Chapter Twenty-One

Dan, walking a little ahead of Red, exchanged a nod with the officer standing outside of Lance Beacon's room on the third floor of the Florida Keys Memorial Hospital. Dan and Red entered. Beacon had a nasal cannula looped over his ears and inserted into his nostrils; an IV line coiled from the fluid bag to the back of his left hand. His neck was swollen and bruised and petechiae dotted his face. His eyes were bugged and the whites were blood red.

"Looking good," Dan said at Beacon's bedside. "You've got kind of a satanic-demon thing going on."

"Fuck you," Beacon said. His voice was raspy.

"That's no way to speak to the guy who's protecting you."

"Protecting me?" Beacon shot back. "You left the front door unlocked."

"Yeah, my bad."

Red snickered.

"Real funny," said Beacon. "I could have been killed."

"But you weren't," Dan reminded him. "Thanks to my good friend, Red, here. He's the one who noticed the car out front."

"What now?" Beacon asked.

"Well, the police are involved now, so maybe he will just let it go or—"

"Or what?"

"Or he might make your death a lot more painful, like he promised."

"What about my family?"

"Already on it," Dan explained. "The chief of police here in Key West has already spoken with the Cutler Bay Police Department and they're watching your family."

"Thank God. So my wife knows everything?"

"I have no idea what they've told her. Why don't you give her a call?"

"I guess I should."

"They say how long you're gonna be in here?" Red asked.

"The doctor said she wants me to stay overnight for observation."

"Okay. You get some rest, Beacon. There's a cop on duty outside your door. You'll be safe here tonight. Red and I have a few things to take care of. We'll be back in the morning to pick you up."

Dan and Red turned and left the room.

"Wow," Red commented. "Getting strangled really frigs up your face."

"That ain't so bad," said Dan. "I've looked worse than that after puking my guts out the morning after a bad drunk."

"That's nothing to brag about."

"Or is it?"

"No."

"Kinda."

"Not at all, pal."

# Chapter Twenty-Two

Dan took a left off of North Roosevelt Boulevard into the Home Depot parking lot. He was driving Bev's minivan. Red was in the passenger seat next to him, and Mel was sitting Indian-style on the floor, in the back. The seats had been removed.

Dan parked, and the three got out and made their way into the building. As soon as they got inside, Dan's cell phone rang. "Hello?"

"It's Joey."

"I was just going to call you," Dan replied. "Hold on." He turned to Red and Mel. "Go to the hardware aisle and grab a small box of 2 ½ inch galvanized screws."

"You got it," Red said.

Dan put the cell back to his ear. "Joey, I gotta speak with Tony."

"About what?" Joey asked.

"I spoke with the bartender at the Wounded Parrot. He gave the same description of the woman and pretty much the same account of what happened as Tony did."

"Well, yeah, I'm sure he did. Did you think Tony was lying?"

"No," Dan replied. "But I was hoping the bartender might remember something Tony didn't … like the woman's name."

"He said he didn't get her name."

"I know, Joey, but ask him again. We got a description of her, but there's a lot of skinny blondes in their thirties down here. A name would help narrow it down."

"I'll talk to him."

"Also, Joey, it would help if you would give me the name of the people he was delivering the money to."

"That's the reason I was calling."

"What do you mean?"

"The man the boys were delivering the money to, he wants to meet you."

"Why does he want to do that?"

"He wants his money back even more than I want my nephew back."

"Does he think Tony and Ricky did something with the money?"

"I hope not, but we would never know if he thought that until it was too late."

"We?"

"We."

"What's the guy's name?"

"I'll have McSwain get back to you with that information, Coast, but be careful."

"Joey, do you think these people had something to do with Ricky's disappearance?"

"I just don't think so, Coast. We've been doing business with these people for a long time. McSwain will get back to you." Joey hung up and Dan slipped the cell back into his pants pocket.

Mel and Red were on their way back down the aisle, each with their own box of screws in hand.

"We only needed one box of screws," Dan said.

"He wouldn't let me carry them, so I got my own," Mel replied.

"Of course you did," said Dan. "Let's get a couple sheets of plywood. "Mel, grab that cart over there."

Mel ran for the cart.

"Ya couldn't just let him carry the screws?" Dan asked.

"I wanted to carry them," Red answered.

"I've never met two people more alike."

"Hey! What's that supposed to mean? He's nuts."

"And you think you're normal?"

"Who's normal?" Mel asked, when he rejoined his pals.

"No one here," Dan replied.

On their way back to the van, Mel pushed the cart.

"Be careful with that," Dan said. "Don't run it into any cars."

"I know what I'm doing," Mel responded. "I used to drive these carts for a living."

Dan's phone rang again. "Hello?"

"Coast, it's McSwain. You got a pen and paper?"

"Yes," Dan lied.

"The man you're going to meet is Eli Marrone. Make sure you're home at four this afternoon."

"Is he going to call me?"

"No, he's coming to your home."

"I don't want these people knowing where I live."

"Trust me, Coast, he already knew where you lived."

"That's scary."

The call ended.

"Who was that?" Red asked.

"McSwain."

"What did he want?"

"He wants me to be home at four."

# Twenty-Three

At three minutes after four Dan was standing on his six-foot fiberglass stepladder with his battery-operated screw gun in his hand. He was just finishing up fastening the second piece of plywood over his broken picture window.

Red was on the inside picking broken shards of glass out of the sash and gently placing them into a large Glad bag, trying not to rip it.

Mel was taking his afternoon nap at Bev's house.

Red looked up at the plywood as Dan was screwing. "You missed the wood!" he hollered.

"What?" Dan yelled back.

"That last screw. It didn't hit anything."

Dan backed the screw out of the wood, raised it two inches, and tried again.

"You got it," Red shouted.

Dan set the screw gun on top of the ladder and climbed down. Just as both feet hit the ground he heard a vehicle pull up behind him. It was a shiny new black Escalade. It came to a stop half in the street, and half on Dan's front lawn.

Both rear doors swung open and a man climbed out of each side. Both men were wearing tan khakis. The larger man wore a light blue Guayabera shirt. The smaller one, but still bigger than Dan, wore a tight black T-shirt. The driver remained in the vehicle and a fourth man, who was sitting in the front passenger side, climbed out and stood near the front of the vehicle, facing the street.

"Dan Coast?" the guy in the black T-shirt asked.

"Uh-huh," Dan responded.

Black T-shirt pointed at the front door. "Inside."

"Okay," said Dan. "But you'll have to excuse the mess."

Neither man replied but followed Dan into his house. Dan turned just as he went inside to see another vehicle, identical to the first, pull up.

Red backed away from the window when he saw the men enter.

"Red, I would like to introduce you to two friends of mine," Dan said.

"Hi, guys," Red said.

Both remained silent. One took a position near the entrance to the kitchen, and the other stood near the hallway.

"They're not very chatty," said Dan.

"Probably shy," Red remarked. "They just gotta get to know us."

Neither man was amused.

131

Seconds later another man, dressed in a gray pinstriped suit, entered; behind him was Eli Marrone.

Marrone was not what Dan or Red had expected. Dan guessed his age at around fifty-five. He wore blue jeans, a white T-shirt, a beige sport coat, and black leather Converse low-tops. Marrone's hair was white and cut short to just stubble.

"Dan Coast? Eli Marrone."

"I know," said Dan. They shook hands.

Marrone's eyes went to the broken front window, then the hole in the couch, and finally the damaged ceiling. "What the fuck happened here?" he asked.

"A red-headed hitman shot up the place and then jumped through my window."

Marrone cocked his head. "Someone put out a contract on you?"

"No," Dan replied.

"This have anything to do with my money?"

"No."

"Where we at with my money?"

Red stepped forward. "So far all we have—"

Marrone put a finger to his lips. "Shh."

Red stopped talking.

"I'm speaking with Mr. Coast right now," Marrone explained. "If I want you to speak, I'll look at you and ask you a question. Understand?"

Red nodded his head.

"Good." Marrone returned his attention to Dan. "Where we at with my money?"

"All we have so far is the description of a woman that Ricky Bianchi may or may not have left the Wounded Parrot with."

"Three days, and that's all you got? Pantucco said you were good at what you do."

"He may have exaggerated," Dan admitted.

"Maybe this other case you're working on, the one with the skinny red headed hitman, is impeding your ability to produce results."

"I don't think so."

"I didn't ask if you thought so. Why is a hitman after your client?"

"It's a long story."

Marrone looked at his gold Rolex. "I have time. Go ahead."

"My client put a contract on his own life."

Marrone's eyes widened. "He hired this hitman himself?"

"Yes."

"Is he mentally retarded?"

"Just stupid, I think," Dan replied.

"And now he's changed his mind, and hired you two to protect him."

"Yes."

Marrone looked around Dan's house once again. He sighed. "Coast, you have seventy-two hours to find my money."

"What happens after seventy-two hours?"

"I kill you, your friend there, and everyone in the Pantucco family."

"Ouch."

"Yeah, ouch," Marrone said. He turned and started toward the door.

"I didn't say he was skinny," Dan said.

Marrone paused and turned. "What?"

"I didn't say the red-headed hitman was skinny."

Marrone grinned. "His name is Melvin Jessup. Unlike you, he *is* very good at what he does. Frankly, I'm surprised you're still alive. My advice to you is to kill him before he gets another chance to kill you."

"And how do I do that?" Dan asked.

"I'll call you." Marrone turned and walked out the door, followed by his goons.

"Bye guys," Dan said.

"So, what now?" Red asked.

"Shh," Dan responded, with a finger to his lips.

# Chapter Twenty-Four

"Come on, Rick," Dan pleaded. "I'm on a time limit here."

He and Red sat on the leather sofa in Chief Carver's office, across from his desk.

Rick glared at his friend. "Why don't you tell me what's going on first," Rick said, "and then maybe I'll talk about loaning out my sketch artist."

"He's not *your* sketch artist," Dan argued. "I just need his name."

"Why don't you put an ad in the paper and hire your own sketch artist?"

"I don't have time. I need someone now."

"Seriously, Rick," Red agreed. "We need someone now."

"Why?" Rick asked.

"I can't tell you," Dan replied.

Rick sighed. "I'm not even supposed to be here today. You know how much work you've created for this department with your bullshit this morning?"

"I'm just gonna guess, and say, *a bunch*."

"Yeah. A bunch."

"Just his name, Rick."

"It's a she, and her name is Charlotte Walker."

"Is she related to the Texas Ranger?" Dan deadpanned.

Rick ignored his moronic friend and pressed the intercom button on his desk phone. "Angie, can you get Char Walker's phone number for Dan?"

"Yes, Chief," Angie replied.

"It'll be at the front desk. Now get the hell out of my office. And don't make me regret this."

"Have you ever?" Red asked.

The two men shut the door behind them.

On the way back to the car, Dan pulled out his cell and dialed Charlotte Walker. He explained that he needed the services of a sketch artist and Rick had referred her.

"What day were you thinking?" she asked.

"Twenty minutes from now."

"I … um. Twenty minutes from now?"

"Yes, or sooner if you're available."

"That's rather short notice, Mr. Coast."

"Call me Dan."

"Okay, Dan. I can meet you on Wednesday, if that's good."

"Hmm. No, that won't be good. I'll be dead on Wednesday."

"Excuse me?"

"Listen, Char, I need a sketch artist right now. It's a matter of life and death ... mostly death. I'll pay you whatever you want."

"I'm sorry, I—"

"*Whatever* you want."

"I want two grand."

"Fine. Give me your address and I'll pick you up in fifteen minutes."

"You said twenty minutes."

"That was five minutes ago." Dan hung up.

"How much did she want?" Red asked.

"Two grand."

Red whistled. "What a mercenary bitch. I hate her already."

# Chapter Twenty-Five

Dan, Red, and Mel picked up Char Walker in front of her home on Harris Avenue. Char was a short brunette. She was what Dan would call chunky. She was what Red would call perfect. When Dan saw Char, he immediately focused on Red's eyes. There it was. Red was love-struck.

"What happened to hating her?" said Dan.

"Shut up."

Red swung open the passenger side door and jumped out of the Porsche. "Here, Ms. Walker," he said. "You sit up front. Here, let me take that for you."

"That's very kind of you." Char handed Red the portfolio folder she was carrying over her shoulder, but hung onto the small bag she was carrying, and got in.

Red held the door until Char was in her seat, and had adjusted the lap of her orchid print sleeveless sundress. Red gently shut the door, and jumped into the backseat with Mel.

Dan extended his hand. "I'm Dan Coast," he said.

Char shook his hand. "Char Walker."

Dan pointed into the backseat. "That's Mel behind me, and Sir Lancelot back there is Red Baxter."

Char noticed Red's flushed face when she turned around to say hi. She smiled, and Red's face grew a shade darker.

Mel stuck his hand between the front seats. "Shapely Char," he greeted. "it's wonderful to meet you."

"Shapely Char?" she asked.

"He does that with everyone," Dan said.

"Okay? I guess."

Dan put the car in drive and headed for the Wounded Parrot.

"So, what exactly are we doing, Dan?" Char asked.

Red jumped in. "We're taking you to the Wounded Parrot, over on Duval. We have an un-sub—that's unknown subject—who was described to us by a bartender there. We need a sketch to show around town."

"I see," said Char. "So you gentlemen are private detectives?"

"Just like Magnum," Mel blurted out.

"Not really private detectives," Dan explained. "We're just helping out a friend."

"Gotcha," Char responded.

"I own Red's Bar and Grill over on Charles Lake Road," Red said proudly.

"Oh, I've been there a couple times," Char said. "Nice place."

Dan wanted to say something snide about Char's exorbitant fee, but held his tongue to spare his lovelorn friend's feelings. "So, Char," he asked, "can you actually make a living sketching pictures of bad guys?"

Char chuckled. "Not quite. I also paint. My work is in a few of the local galleries. I also work as a barista at the Island Coffee house on Summerland Key."

"That sounds exciting," said Red. "A woman of many talents."

"Serving coffee isn't much of a talent, but it was exciting a few days ago. There was a shooting right across the street."

"You don't say," Dan responded.

"Imagine that," said Red.

Dan pulled the car to the curb. "Here we are," he announced.

Red quickly jumped out of the convertible and pulled open Char's door. "There ya go," he said.

"Thank you," Char said.

Red grabbed her portfolio out of the back seat. "Let me carry this for you."

"You're such a gentleman."

"He sure is," Dan agreed.

Red shot him a look.

As Char started walking down the street toward the Wounded Parrot, Red leaned in to Dan. "She's mine," the big guy said.

Dan put up his hands. "She's all yours," he agreed.

"Who's whose?" Mel questioned.

"Never mind," Red replied. He hurried to open the door for Char.

Dan went through the door behind Char. "Don't overdo it," he said.

"Overdo it?' Red asked. "When have I ever over done it with a woman?"

"Well, there was the time—"

"Shut up."

"Can I have some money for the jukebox?" Mel asked, on his way through.

Dan was first to the bar. A different guy was making drinks. "Excuse me," Dan asked. "Is Albert here?"

"Albert who?" the bartender asked.

"The Albert who works here," Dan replied.

"There's two Alberts who work here."

"Are ya shittin' me?"

"No. Why?"

"Tall guy with a shaved head."

"Yeah, he's in the back."

"Can you tell him Dan Coast would like to speak with him again?"

The bartender sighed loudly and rolled his eyes. "I guess."

"Can I get some money for the jukebox?" Mel asked loudly. A few patrons gazed at him lazily.

"What the Christ?" Dan reached into his pocket and pulled out a five. "Here. That's all you get."

"Sor-*ee*," said Mel, and hurried to the jukebox.

Char placed her folder of the bar and her bag on one of the barstools.

A few seconds later Albert walked through the doorway behind the bar. He pointed at Dan. "The guy from the other day."

Dan pointed back. "You got it."

"I didn't remember anything else, if that's why you're here."

Shirley Temple's "On the Good Ship Lollipop" began playing.

Dan glanced up at one of the speakers that was mounted on a support beam, and shook his head. "No." He pointed to Char. "I brought a police sketch artist. I was wondering if you could sit down with her for a few minutes and maybe she could come up with a sketch we could pass around."

"You said you weren't a cop."

"I'm not."

"Then why you gots a police sketch artist?"

"They loaned her to me."

"Huh, that's nice of 'em. But I'm working. Can we do it tomorrow sometime?"

"No. It's gotta be now." Dan reached back into his pocket for his money clip. He pulled out a hundred-dollar bill and handed it to Albert. "Will a Benjamin do it?"

"Delbert! I'm goin' on break!" Albert shouted as he made his way around the bar.

*Albert, Delbert, and Albert?* Dan wondered. *Huh.*

"You just had a break!" Delbert hollered back from the kitchen.

"Shut up! I'm takin' another one." Albert pointed at a four top table across the room. "That table okay?" he asked.

Char grabbed her sketchpad out of the portfolio and her pencils out of her bag. "Looks good to me," she replied.

Albert and Char took their seats on opposite sides of the table. Dan, Red, and Mel took seats at the bar.

"I need a drink," Dan said.

"Me too," said Red.

"Can I have a Shirley Temple, Dan?" Mel asked. "I can drink ginger ale, and there's just a little squirt of grenadine."

"Did the song remind you of that?" Dan asked.

"What song?" Mel asked.

"'On the Good Ship Lollipop.' You just played it on the jukebox."

"Oh. Yeah, I love that song. Is it about ginger ale?"

"Jesus Christ, Mel. Yeah, it's a song all about ginger ale."

Red laughed out loud.

"I guess I'll have to listen to the words more carefully next time," said Mel. "I just like it because of the beat."

Delbert walked back into the room. "What can I get for you gentlemen?" he asked.

"Tequila, Seven, and lime," Dan ordered. "And a gun."

"I'll just take a look at the wine list," Mel said.

# Chapter Twenty-Six

It was a good forty-five minutes and three drinks later before Dan heard Albert shout, "That's her! That's the woman."

Dan got up from the bar and walked over to the table. Red followed him. They looked over Char's shoulder at the drawing.

"Look familiar?" Char asked.

"Nobody I know," Dan answered.

"Me neither," said Red.

Dan looked at Albert. "You think this looks a lot like her?" he asked.

"It looks exactly like her," Albert assured him.

Char tore the page out of her pad and handed it to Dan.

Dan stared at it a second longer and then said, "Let's get you home, Char." He turned to Red. "Then we'll stop by OfficeMax and get a few copies of this made up."

"What about my money?" Char asked.

"It's Saturday, Char. I don't have that kind of money on me."

"I'll take a check."

"I don't own a checkbook."

Char looked surprised. "Is he kidding?"

Red shook his head. "Sadly, he's not. He didn't even have debit card till a year ago."

"Well then, let's go to the ATM," suggested Char.

"Don't know my PIN number," Dan said ashamedly.

"How much you have on you?" Char asked.

Dan took out his money clip and fanned through the bills. "A little over six hundred."

She snatched it out of his hand. "You can pay me the rest first thing Monday morning."

"He has an AA meeting first thing Monday morning," Red said.

"Broke and a drunk," said Char. "That's great."

"I'm not broke," Dan said.

"He's just a drunk," Red assured her.

Char shook her head and gathered up her things. "I'll see you at the car."

"You were right the first time," said Dan when he was out of earshot. "She is a mercenary bitch."

"Better watch your mouth, Coast," Red bristled. "That's the woman I'm going to marry."

Dan saw the dreamy look in his friend's eyes and bit his tongue.

*****

After Dan dropped Char back off at her house, the three men headed for OfficeMax. Dan found a spot near the building and they went inside.

"Excuse me," Dan said to the first employee he saw. "I'm looking for a Xerox machine."

The young man gave him a condescending grin. "A Xerox m*achine*?" he asked.

"Yes. I need to run off some photocopies of this sketch."

"Right this way." The young man turned and walked over to the photocopier. "Here you go," he said, with the wave of an arm. He watched as Dan, Mel, and Red stood before the Xerox WorkCentre 7855 with bewildered looks upon their faces.

"Um, you know how to run one of these things?" Dan asked.

"It might as well be the flight controls aboard the Space Shuttle," Red admitted.

"They discontinued the Space Shuttle program in 2011, Red," Mel interjected authoritatively.

"Very good," said Dan. "You really aren't as crazy as you look, are you?"

Mel beamed. "Why, no, Dan. Thank you very much."

Red chuckled. "I doubt they discontinued the whole Space Shuttle program, Mel," Red said, making finger quotes around the word discontinued.

"They did discontinue the Shuttle program, sir," confirmed the young man impatiently. "Do you need me to make the copies for you?"

"That would be great," Dan said. "Does this thing make them in color?"

"Yeah."

"Nice."

On their way back to the car, Dan handed half the stack of copies to Red, and kept the other half for himself.

"There," Dan said. "You can walk down the east side of Duval and Mel and I will walk down the west side. Take the photo into every bar and restaurant you pass, and ask if they recognize her. Also ask if you can leave one of the copies to put on their bulletin board."

"You would think someone would recognize her," Red said.

"We have to walk all the way down Duval Street?" Mel complained. "Can't we take the car? It's the longest street in the world."

"Mel," Red said, "that's just a figure of speech."

"How do you figure?" Mel asked.

"Shut up and get in the car," Dan said. "Both of you."

Dan found a parking spot on Greene Street and the three men walked the block to Duval.

Red looked up the street one way and down the other. "Might as well start at Bagatelle," he decided.

"And we'll start at the Smallest Bar," Dan said. He stepped off the curb. "Come on, Mel."

"I want to go with Red," Mel argued.

"Come on, Mel," Dan repeated sternly.

"Fine," said Mel.

One by one Dan, Mel, and Red hit every bar from one end of Duval Street to the other. They showed every bartender and many of the patrons at each bar the photo of the unknown blonde. Every time, the answer was pretty much the same: "Never seen her before in my life," and "She don't look familiar to me."

Dan and Mel finished their trek at the Cork and Stogie. As they walked down the steps to the sidewalk, Mel said, "Well, that was a big waste of time."

Dan gave his friend a look. "I don't think it was a complete waste of time," he said.

"Not one person knew her."

"Yeah, that's weird."

"Maybe she's a ghost."

"Yeah, maybe," Dan responded sarcastically.

"She could be. I was watching *Ghost Hunters* the other day and—"

"*Ghost Hunters* isn't real, Mel."

Mel snickered. "Yeah, okay. *Ghost Hunters* isn't real. Then why do they call it reality TV? Reality means real."

"I guess you got me there, Mel."

"You guessed right."

Dan looked up and down Duval Street. "Where the hell is Red?" he wondered aloud.

"Maybe he had better luck than us," said Mel.

"Let's hope so." Dan squinted and tried to focus on the big guy stumbling toward them. "What the Christ?"

Mel stretched his neck to see where Dan was looking. "Is that—"

"Yeah."

Red staggered down the opposite sidewalk like a hairless Sasquatch on a bender. When he saw Dan and Mel across the street from him, he stopped, gave them two thumbs up and a drunken grin, and shouted, "Wooooo!"

"I think he's drunk," Mel said.

"What makes you say that?" Dan asked.

"A bunch of things."

"Hey, guys!" Red hollered. "How did you make out with the blonde lady? Nobunny I talked to ever sawed her before!"

Dan and Mel crossed the street. "What the Christ happened to you?" Dan asked.

"Well, I had one drink at Irish Kevin's. Then a little while later I had one at Fogarty's. I had one at Fat Tuesday's and then a couple at Willie T's. Then I got to—"

"Okay, I get the idea," Dan said. "We gotta get you back to the car."

"I can walk," Red argued. "We'll hit a couple places on the way back." He hung on his two friends for support.

"We're not hitting anything on the way back."

"I'm getting hungry," Mel said.

"We'll eat after we take this drunk home."

"I could eat," Red said.

Dan pointed. "Mel, stop that cab."

Mel stepped off the curb and threw up his arm. The cab came to a stop next to them. Dan opened the back door and helped Red inside.

"He ain't gonna puke in here I hope," the driver warned.

"He's fine," Dan said.

"He don't look fine," said the driver.

"I would imagine you've seen worse."

"I guess. Where ya headed?"

"Back the other way," Dan answered. "The corner of Duval and Greene."

"You got it," said the driver.

Mel climbed in the front seat and Dan jumped in the back with his drunken buddy.

"You still got Charlotte's number?" Red asked. He leaned over and put his head on Dan's shoulder.

"Yeah," Dan replied. "Why?"

"She's really purdy. I think I should call her. Where's my cell phone?"

"Let's wait until tomorrow to do that," Dan suggested.

"Red's got a girlfriend," Mel sang.

"Ha! Red's got a girlfriend," Red sang along. "Let's call her."

"You're too drunk for that, pal," Dan said. "We'll call her tomorrow."

"That's a good idea, Dan. You're such a good friend. You're my best friend."

"What about me?" Mel asked.

"You're my second best friend, Mel."

"Nice," said Mel.

"We'll call her tomorrow," Red said. He closed his eyes and his head fell forward.

"You know what," Dan said to the driver. "Go ahead and take us over to Rose Street to his house, then I only have to get him out of the car once."

The driver flipped on his blinker. "You got it, pal."

"And then can we get something to eat?" Mel asked, as he stared skyward out the passenger side window.

"Yes," Dan responded.

"And I need to take my medication."

"Crap. I forgot. We'll get that too."

Mel started singing "talkin' 'bout my medication" to the tune of the Who's "My Generation" while slapping out a manic drumbeat on the dashboard.

The driver looked apprehensively in his rearview mirror at Dan. "He okay?"

"On his planet, he's considered normal," Dan replied.

# Chapter Twenty-Seven

It was a little before four the following morning when the vibration of Dan's phone caused it to dance across the top of his nightstand. He was already awake, just lying there deep in thought about the blonde woman nobody seemed to know. He rolled over and grabbed the cell. The number appearing on the screen was new to him.

"Hello?" said Dan.

"Melvin Jessup is staying at the Laguna Motel. He's probably sound asleep, so I would get over there as quick as I could."

"I thought maybe *you* would do something about him," Dan said hopefully.

"He's not my problem, he's yours. Take care of it."

"What room is—"

*Click.*

"—he in?"

Dan jumped out of bed and dialed his phone as he hurried to Mel's room.

"Yeah?" Red asked.

"You up?" Dan asked. He pushed open the door to Mel's room. "Get up, Mel." He grabbed Mel's leg and shook it.

Mel stirred.

"Huh?" Red asked.

"Are you awake?" Dan asked.

"I don't even think I'm alive," Red responded. He coughed, and cleared his throat. "Why, what's the matter?"

"Mel, get up!" Dan said, with a little more urgency in his voice.

"I'll pick you up in ten minutes," Dan said.

"Aw, come on," Red pleaded.

"Just get dressed and be ready when I get there."

"Ready for what?"

"Ten minutes." Dan hung up. "Get out of bed, Mel, and get dressed."

Mel swung his legs over the edge of the bed. "What's wrong?" he said blearily.

"Nothing. We have to go for a drive."

Mel sat next to Boozer and stroked his back. "Can I bring Boozer?" he asked.

"No. He'll be fine. We won't be gone that long." Dan ran back to his room and put on his shorts. He grabbed a T-shirt from his drawer and put that on as well. On his way back down the hall he went into the bathroom, took a leak, and splashed a few handfuls of water on his face.

Dan hurried out of the bathroom and back to Mel's room. Mel was gone and Boozer was curled up on his pillow.

"Where the Christ did he go, dog?" Dan asked.

Dan went into the living room and to the front door, he could see Mel sitting in the front seat of the Porsche. Dan grabbed his car keys and ran out the door.

"You're still in your pajamas," Dan commented, as he climbed into the driver's seat.

"I'll just wait in the car," Mel said.

Dan glanced down at Mel's feet to make sure he was wearing shoes; he was wearing his slippers. *Good enough*, Dan thought and backed out of the driveway.

"Where we going?" Mel asked.

"The Laguna Hotel," Dan replied. The tires squealed as Dan rounded the corner onto George Street.

"You're driving too fast."

"I know."

"You're going to lose your license again."

"No I'm not."

"You're going to get a ticket."

"No I'm not."

Dan pulled to the curb in front of Red's; the big man was nowhere in sight. Dan thought about honking, but it was still dark and he didn't want to wake Red's neighbors.

"You want me to go in and get him?" Mel asked.

"You just stay right where you are," Dan replied.

"Honk the horn."

"No."

Red's front door swung open and out walked the bow-legged man. Red was moving slowly and held a can of Pepsi against his forehead. "I feel like shit," he said when he reached the car.

"You look like shit," Dan responded.

"Thanks. Can I sit in the front, Mel?"

"I want to sit in the front," Mel said.

Red didn't feel like arguing. He climbed over the driver's side door and fell into the backseat, head first. Dan put the car in drive and spun the tires.

"Take it easy!" Red shouted. "Unless you want me to puke all over your backseat."

Dan ignored the request and slid sideways around the corner onto Ashby Street, slamming red against the door.

"Oh, shit!" Red groaned. "It's coming up!"

"Swallow hard," Dan ordered.

# Chapter Twenty-Eight

Dan steered to the edge of the street and rolled to a stop about a half of a block down from the Laguna Motel.

The Laguna Motel was a small one-story, thirty-room dive frequented by addicts and anyone else looking to pay by the hour. There was a parking lot with a string of sixteen rooms on one side and fourteen on the other. At the far end of the fourteen rooms was a small office, and behind those rooms was an algae-encrusted pool, home to a few brave frogs that lived in puddles of rainwater, that hadn't seen chlorinated water for decades. In the fifties and sixties the Laguna had welcomed scores of vacationing families, but those days were long behind her.

Red righted himself in the seat and took a look around. "What are we doing here?" he asked.

"Melvin Jessup is staying here," Dan replied.

"Who the hell is Melvin Jessup?" Red asked.

"The red-headed hitman."

"Oh yeah. How do you know that?"

"Eli Marrone just called me and told me."

"And?"

"He wants us to take care of him."

"Take care of him? What did he mean, take care of him?"

"Duh, Red," Mel said. "He wants us to kill him."

"I'm not killing anybody," Red said.

Mel pushed open his door. "Where's your gun, Dan?" he asked. "I'll do it."

"Get back in here," Dan scolded. "Nobody's killin' anybody."

"You never let me do anything fun," Mel complained.

"I just want to make sure he's really here before I call Rick," Dan explained.

"Call Rick," Red repeated. "Good idea."

The trio got out of the car and made their way toward the office.

"We're just gonna walk in there?" Red asked. "What if he sees us?"

"He's probably sleeping," Dan said.

"It's always hope, maybe, and probably with you."

Dan got to the office first. He pulled open the door and stood back for Red to enter.

"No, no," Red said. "After you."

Dan went in and walked up to the desk. An old woman in her mid-eighties sat in a rocking chair watching an old tube television; a White Owl cigar dangled from the corner of her mouth. She didn't notice the three men enter. Dan stared at her waiting for a response. He glanced back at Red and Mel; they both shrugged.

Dan tapped the service bell that was sitting on the counter. "Excuse me," he said.

The old woman jumped and grabbed her chest. Her cigar fell from her mouth and bounced off her saggy breasts, hitting the floor in front of her. "Jesus Christ!" she shouted. "Never sneak up on an old woman like that."

"Sorry," Dan said. "I thought you heard—"

"Well, I didn't." Several of the woman's joints cracked as she got out of the chair, bent over, and picked up her stogie. She laid the wet, chewed-up cigar on the edge of the counter. "Rooms are forty bucks an hour … each. I don't care what weird shit the three of you do to each other in there, but keep it down."

"We don't want a room," Dan explained. "We just want some information."

"What happens here, stays here. Just like Vegas. Y'all won't get no information from me."

Dan looked around the seedy room. "Well, not *just* like Vegas," he said.

"Watch it, smart-ass," the old hag warned. "This here motel been in my family a long time."

"We just want to know if someone is staying here," Red explained. "Skinny red-headed guy in his thirties."

"He's a hitman," Mel added.

"A hitman? In my place?"

"Is he here?" Dan asked.

"He's here. Room fourteen." The old woman turned and grabbed a room key off a rack full of keys.

Dan snatched the key from her hand. "What are you doing?" he asked.

"Gonna throw him out on his ass, that's what I'm doin'. Don't need that kinda element around my place."

"We're gonna call the cops," Dan insisted.

"I don't want no goddamn cops here either."

"He's a hired killer," Red said. "You can't go in there by yourself."

The old woman pushed past Dan, and Red grabbed her by the shoulders.

"Help!" she cried out. "Rape!"

Red put his hand over her mouth. "Shut up, ya old bat," he said.

She was trying her damnedest to scream from behind Red's massive hand.

Dan pulled out his cell and dialed Rick's number.

"What now?" Rick answered.

"It's Dan. I'm at the Laguna Motel. Melvin Jessup is here."

Rick cleared his throat. "Who the hell is Melvin Jessup?" he asked.

"The hitman who went through my window."

"Holy crap!" Rick shouted. "What's he doing there? What are you doing there?"

"Just get here." Dan sidestepped to the door and looked down the walkway. "His room is dark. He's probably still asleep."

"Don't do anything," Rick ordered. "I'll be right there."

Within ten minutes the entire Laguna Motel was surrounded by what looked like the entire Key West Police Department. Two units were parked sideways at each end of the street, blocking traffic. Two more units were parked on the lawn, behind the pool, and watching the rear entrance to room fourteen. A unit was parked at the entrance to the motel; Rick's Bronco, along with another patrol car, was parked in the parking lot. Several of the officers had evacuated the other rooms and now took positions behind patrol cars with their weapons drawn. The old woman had been taken to a safe location down the street with the motel guests. Dan had to hand it to Rick for his professionalism. The units had approached the motel with their lights turned off, and the evacuation had been conducted with stealth and precision, so as not to alert Jessup. The few guests—which included prostitutes and their johns—had cooperated without raising a fuss when Rick's men assured them they wouldn't be busted. Room 13, next door to Jessup's, was occupied, but the guest was not disturbed out of an abundance of caution.

Dan, Mel, and Red stood with Chief Carver behind his Bronco; Carver was gripping a bullhorn. The sun had come up, but there was still no movement from Jessup's room.

"Are you positive he's in there?" Rick asked.

"That's what the old lady said," Red replied.

"What made you come here?" Rick asked.

"I can't say," said Dan.

Rick put the bullhorn to his mouth and pressed the mic trigger. "This is Chief Rick Carver with the Key West Police Department," he said. "Melvin Jessup, if you're in there, I want you to come out slowly, with your hands in the air."

"Like you just don't care!" Red sang out.

Dan shot him a grin.

"I think I'm still a little drunk," said Red.

"And still a little stupid," Rick mumbled.

Everyone on the scene stared at the door to room number fourteen. Suddenly the door to room number thirteen opened. The cops aimed their weapons. Billy Maple walked through the door, stretching his arms above him and yawning.

"Hey, Billy!" Mel shouted, and waved.

"Hey, Mel!" Billy hollered back. "What's going on?"

"There's a hired killer in the room next door to you, but he won't come out."

"Cool." Billy stepped back inside the room and shut the door.

"What the Christ is that idiot doing?" Dan asked.

A minute later Billy's door opened again. He walked out the door, across the parking lot, and stood next to Mel. "This is exciting," he said.

"I know," Mel agreed. "Dan and Red do all kinds of cool things."

"Just stay down," Rick said, and returned the bullhorn to his lips. "Melvin Jessup, this is your last chance. If you don't come out, we're coming in." Rick released the trigger and laid the bullhorn on the hood of the Bronco.

"How the hell are we gonna get him out of there?" Dan asked.

"He'll be out soon enough," Billy said matter-of-factly.

"Why do you say that?" Red asked.

"Do you smell smoke?" Rick asked, sniffing the air.

Dan pointed at Billy's room. "The curtains are on fire!"

"You ain't seen nothin' yet," Billy said. He plugged his ears, turned around, and squatted down, putting his back against Rick's rear tire. "I unscrewed the hose that goes to the stove too."

"Shit!" Dan shouted. "Get down!"

"Get down!" Rick shouted. "Get down!"

Everyone took cover.

The explosion blew out every window in the motel, as well as Rick's driver's side windows, and a few windows in other patrol cars. The mushroom cloud rose at least fifty feet in the air. Shards of glass, wood, and every other material used in the construction of the motel rained down on the crowd.

When the debris settled, everyone got to their feet. Rooms twelve, thirteen, and fourteen were fully engulfed in flames.

"It's beautiful," Billy said, gazing upon his fiery creation. He ground his fist into his hand like a mad scientist. "Glorious."

Jessup's door swung open, and out he ran, firing his sawed-off shotgun in one hand and a pistol in the other. He looked like a skinny, red-headed, two-eyed Rooster Cogburn.

Several officers, including Rick, began firing.

Jessup pulled the revolver's trigger until it was empty, and then pulled it four more times. He dropped to his knees, and then went face first into the blacktop parking lot.

"Hold your fire!" Rick shouted.

Two officers ran to Jessup, their weapons still drawn, and trained on the young man.

"Ya think he's dead?" Mel asked.

"He's dead," Rick replied.

"You're welcome," said Billy Maple.

# Chapter Twenty-Nine

Dan, Red, and Mel sat in one of the old wooden booths at Pepe's Cafe. Dan got two eggs over medium with bacon, home fries, and an English muffin. Red got the same thing, but with scrambled eggs. Mel ordered a cheese omelet.

"I can't believe Rick tried to blame that fire on me," Dan said. He blew into his mug of coffee and then took a sip. "That Billy Maple is in no way my responsibility."

"You did show us how to escape," Mel reminded him.

"No, I showed *you* how to escape. You showed him. This is kinda your fault."

"You don't think I'm going to get into trouble, do you?"

"You can just plead insanity."

"You think the jury would buy it?"

"I don't think you'd have anything to worry about."

"I would probably represent myself in court."

"Oh yeah?" said Red. "You think that would be a good idea?"

"Of course," Mel replied. "I used to be a wealthy playboy lawyer in Los Angeles … that is until I was wounded and had to spend the rest of my life in a wheelchair."

Red cocked his head. "So, you were kinda like Perry Mason?"

Mel snickered. "Don't be ridiculous, Red. I was more like Robert Ironside."

"I think you're getting two different shows mixed up there, Mel," Dan pointed out.

"What do you mean, shows?" Mel asked.

"If he brings Godzilla into this discussion …" said Red.

"How about if we end this discussion," Dan suggested.

"Maybe you're right." Red glanced up at the clock that hung on the wall over the door, underneath the exit sign. "After all, we've only got about fifty-six hours to live."

"Don't remind me," Dan said.

"So what do we do next?" Red asked. "I thought for sure somebody in one of those bars would have recognized the blonde lady."

"Me too," said Dan.

"Maybe she's not really blonde," Mel offered. "And maybe she doesn't usually go to bars."

"The bartender and Tony Bianchi both said she was blonde," Dan said.

"Maybe she was wearing a wig."

"Why would she be wearing a wig?" Red asked.

"Maybe she's an actress, like that woman that got killed the other day," Mel said.

"What woman?" Dan asked.

"The woman who got hit by a car on Flagler Avenue last week. Wow, Dan, don't you listen to anything I say? The person just hit her and left her in the road to die. Who would do that?"

"How do you know she was an actress?" Red asked.

"I read about her in the paper," Mel answered. "She had a husband and a little girl, and she was a stay-at-home mom, and she acted in plays."

Mel didn't usually play with a full deck, but Dan recognized he was now in one of his focused lucid phases. "What plays?" he asked.

"At the Waterfront Theater."

"What makes you think the woman who got hit by the car wore wigs?" Dan asked.

"The picture in the paper showed a wig lying in the street next to the curb," Mel replied. "At first I thought it was her head, but then I figured they wouldn't put that in the paper."

"Probably not," said Dan.

"What color was the wig?" Red asked.

"It looked like a blonde wig," Mel responded.

Dan raised his hand. "Check, please!"

# Chapter Thirty

Dan, Red, and Mel sat on barstools at Red's Bar and Grill. Cindy, the bartender, stood behind the bar polishing glasses.

"You guys want something to drink?" Cindy asked.

"Ginger ale," Dan replied.

"Coffee," said Red. "And some aspirins."

"Water please," Mel ordered.

"There's no way Rick is going to just give us that woman's address," Red said. "Not without a bunch of questions anyway."

"The funeral home would have the address," Dan commented. "They probably won't give it out either."

"The theater would have it," said Mel.

"I'm sure we wouldn't be able to get a hold of anyone on Sunday," Dan pointed out.

"Same goes for my buddy Garcia over at the DMV," said Red. "I can give him a call tomorrow after they open."

"We'll only have thirty-six hours to live at that point," Dan said.

Cindy set their drinks in front of them one by one. "Thirty-six hours to live?" she asked.

"It's a long story," Red said.

Dan's cell phone rang. "Hello?"

"What do ya got for me?" Joey Pantucco asked.

"Hey, Joey! I was just going to call you."

"You were, were you?"

"Yeah. How quickly can you get an address for me?"

"This have something to do with my nephew?"

"Yup."

"It shouldn't take long. What's his name?"

"It's a her."

"What's her name?"

Dan turned to Mel. "What's the woman's name?"

"What woman?" Mel asked.

"The woman who got hit by the car, for Christ sakes."

"I have no idea."

"Are ya shittin' me? You knew everything about her. But you don't know her name?"

"Sorry. I don't remember her name."

"Joey, I'm gonna have to call you back." Dan hung up the phone before Joey had a chance to respond. "Red, you got Thursday's newspaper around here somewhere?"

"Should be in the recyclables in the back," Red replied. "Or you could just look the article up online."

"Screw that, too much trouble." Dan swung his leg over the stool. "Come on, let's look for it."

"Hold on," Red said. He unscrewed the cap from the aspirin bottle, took six of the little white tablets, and washed it down with a mouthful of coffee.

Red was halfway through the kitchen door when Cindy said. "Oh, yeah, Red, someone called for you this morning."

"Who was it?" Red asked.

"A Charlotte Walker."

Red spun around. He was grinning from ear to ear. "You shittin' me?"

"No."

"Did Dan put you up to this? You bustin' my balls?"

"I'm not busting your balls."

"What did she want?"

"She didn't say. She just left a number where she could be reached. It's right there by the register."

The smiled faded from Red's face as he turned and made his way through the kitchen. "That's just great," he mumbled. "I'll probably be dead in two days, and now women start calling me."

By the time Red got out behind the building, Dan was boosting Mel into the dumpster.

"You're making *him* go in?" Red asked.

"He begged me," Dan replied. "Up ya go."

Mel went up and over the edge, landing head first in the container. "What am I looking for?" he asked, popping his head up like a meerkat.

"A newspaper," Dan replied.

"There's a lot of newspapers in here."

"We want Thursday's." Dan turned to Red. "After Joey gets us this woman's address, we'll go speak to the husband. Maybe he can tell us where she was last Sunday."

"And if someone hired her for an acting job," Red added.

"Exactly."

The back door opened and Cindy poked her head out. She waved a folded newspaper in the air. "Is this the paper you were looking for?" she asked.

Red walked over and took it from her. He read the date at the top of the front page. "That's it," he said. "Thanks."

"Nice," Dan said, and they walked back inside.

"Dan!" Mel called out. "Hey, Dan! I'm still in here."

When they got back to the bar Dan called Joey Pantucco."

"Hello?" Joey answered.

"I got the woman's name," Dan said.

"Go ahead."

"It's Maria Blair."

"Maria Blair," Joey repeated. "You just need an address?"

"Yes. As quick as possible."

"Maria Blair," Joey said once more. "That name sounds familiar."

"Do you think she's someone you know?" Dan asked.

"I don't know. It just sounds familiar."

"Maybe one of your nephews mentioned her name in the past."

"You think she's the woman Ricky left with?"

"I think she's connected in some way."

"I'll call you back as soon as I get the address." Joey hung up.

Dan laid his phone on the bar. He glanced up at the clock over the back bar. "I hope this doesn't take too long."

"Yeah me too," Red agreed.

Mel pushed open the kitchen door. "Thanks a lot," he said angrily.

"Where the hell were you?" Dan asked.

"In the dumpster."

Dan laughed. "Oh yeah. Sorry about that."

"Sorry about that," Mel aped. He added, "I got to go water my mule."

Mel breezed past Dan on his way to the john. Dan noticed there was something on Mel's backside.

"Uh, Mel, there's a French fry stuck to your ass," Dan called out.

Mel froze. "Oh, thanks." He craned his big paw around, snagged the ketchupy fry, and popped it into his mouth. "Yummy."

"Now I am gonna throw up," said Red.

# Chapter Thirty-One

Joey Pantucco got back to Dan in less than two hours with the address of the late Maria Blair. Dan, Red, and Mel climbed in Dan's car and headed for the house.

"I feel kinda funny going over there like this," Red said. "I mean, she just died a few days ago."

"We have no choice," Dan said. He pointed at his glove box. "Open that up and hand me a few of those business cards."

Red pushed the button and the door dropped open. He reached inside, counted out about eight of the business cards, and handed the small stack to Dan. "Here ya go," he said.

Dan's business cards were nothing more than an antique white card with his name, cell phone number; underneath his name was the word investigator. Dan had discovered that putting "investigator" on a business card was perfectly legal in Florida, as long as the word private, or licensed wasn't written before it, and you didn't claim to be licensed. After all, anyone who inquired about anything was technically an investigator. Dan just had to make sure that any money that exchanged hands was untraceable.

Dan pulled to the curb across the street from the gray single-story home at 3632 Eagle Avenue. A young girl with long brown braids sat on the front steps. Her elbows were on her knees and her chin rested in her palms. "This must be it," he commented. As he climbed from the vehicle he pulled out his money clip and slid the business cards inside. "Come on, Red. Mel, you wait in the car."

"Aw, man," Mel shot back. "Why do I have to wait in the car?"

"Because I said so." As Dan neared the house, he saw the little girl smile, raise her arm, and give a little wave.

Dan turned around. Mel was smiling back at the little girl and waving.

"Excuse me," said Dan. "Is your daddy at home?"

The kid nodded. "Yes, sir."

"We were wondering if we could speak with him."

The ten-year-old stood, turned, and walked up the steps. She opened the door and hollered, "Dad!"

"What is it Julia?" came a voice from inside the house.

"Two guys are here to talk to you."

Seconds late a man appeared at the door with a concerned look on his face. "Can I help you?" he asked.

Dan reached inside his pocket and retrieved the money clip. "Sorry to bother you on a Sunday like this, Mr. Blair." Dan handed the man his card. "We're working with the Waterfront Theater. I'm Mr. Coast, and this is my associate, Mr. Baxter."

Red, standing behind Dan and one step lower, nodded when he was introduced. He had his hands folded in front of him and tried his best to appear somber.

"Is this about my wife?" Blair asked.

"Yes, and let me say we're very sorry about your loss," Dan replied. He glanced down at the little ears that were taking it all in. "Would it be okay if we spoke inside?"

"Sure. Come on in." Blair pulled the door all the way open. "Julia, can you stay out here for a little while?"

"Yes, Dad."

Julia sat back down on the steps; the three men went inside and shut the door behind them.

"Please, have a seat," Blair said. He pointed at the two chairs against the front wall. Dan sat in one and Red the other.

"So, what's this all about?"

"Awhile back, Mr. Blair—"

"Call me Jack."

"Very well, Jack. Your wife took out a small life insurance policy on herself, through the theater company."

Red gave Dan a look, trying his best not to seem confused.

"You were named as the beneficiary," Dan said.

"I had no idea," said Blair. "She never mentioned it."

"We just have a few questions," Dan said. He took out his cell phone and pretended to read while tapping the screen.

"Your date of birth, Jack?" Dan asked.

"October third, 1975."

"And your middle name, Jack?"

"Evan."

"The police report said hit-and-run."

Blair shook his head yes. His eyes went to an eight-by-ten photograph of him and his wife that sat on a wooden mantel attached to the wall below the television.

"No one has been charged?" Dan asked

"No," said Blair

"Your wife—"

"Maria."

"Of course, Maria. Maria was walking along Flagler Avenue. Is that right?" Dan continued to stare at the dark blank screen of his phone.

"She was *crossing* Flagler," Blair corrected.

"Where was she going?" Red asked.

"She was coming home," said Blair, "from her cousin's house, over on Sunrise Lane."

"Is her cousin also in the theater group?" Dan asked.

"No. Well, yes. She doesn't act. She volunteers as a stage hand. Set design, things like that."

"Were they close?" Red asked.

"Well, yes and no," Blair explained. His eyes went back to the photograph. "Janet was always a little jealous of Maria. Even though they got along, there was always an underlying tension between them."

Dan looked at the photograph of Maria and her husband. "Your wife was very beautiful."

"Thank you," said Blair, "and so smart and talented as well. I suppose that's where the tension came from between her and Janet."

"How so?" Red asked.

"Janet was never as pretty as Maria growing up, or as talented." Blair grinned. "But we won't feel too sorry for Janet. She's done quite well for herself."

"What do you mean?" Dan asked.

"She married very well. Her husband's family had money. Her father in-law was some big shot lawyer out west—LA, I think. Had a big law firm out there. Janet's husband is a financial adviser. One of his brothers is chief of staff at a hospital in New York City, and the other is an attorney in Miami. They all did well, and then when the old man passed away, they inherited quite a bit."

"Sounds like Janet hit the lottery," Dan said.

"Her money was the only thing she had over Maria, and she never missed an opportunity to let Maria know it."

"How do you mean?" Dan asked.

"Well, this one time, Janet's housekeeper quit, so Janet offered Maria the job. I knew she only did it so she could boss Maria around, but Maria wanted to take the job to help out her cousin. I talked her out of it, of course. She even hired her last week for a little acting gig. Nothing big. She just wanted Maria to help her play a joke on a couple guys who were in town for the day."

Dan and Red looked at each other and then back at Blair. "Do you know who the guys were?" Dan asked.

"No, I didn't know them. I guess they were clients of Grant's—that's Janet's husband—and he wanted to play a little joke on them to get even for something they did to him. It was all in good fun Maria said."

"Would you be able to give us Janet's address?"

"Why would you need that?" Blair asked.

"We would just like to ask her a few questions."

"That seems odd."

"If Maria's death was in any way connected to her work with the theater, acting, and whatnot," Red explained, "the policy pays double."

Dan's eyes widened and he shot Red a look.

"Isn't that right, Mr. Coast?" Red asked.

"Yes, Mr. Baxter," Dan responded. "It is."

"Oh." Blair stood, and left the room. When he returned, he was holding a yellow Post-it note on which he had written, JANET TROXLER: 3726 SUNRISE LN., and handed the note to Dan. "There you go."

"Thank you for your time, Jack," Dan said, taking the address. "And once again, we're very sorry for your loss."

When Dan and Red walked back outside, Mel was seated on the steps next to Julia; they were both laughing. Mel turned and saw Dan and Red coming through the door.

"Well, I have to go now, Julia," Mel said. "It was very nice to meet you."

Julia reached out to shake Mel's hand. "It was nice to meet you too, Mel."

The three men returned to Dan's car and left.

"What were you talking to the kid about?" Dan asked.

"I told her about how I lost my mom when I was about her age," Mel replied, a might sadly.

"I didn't know about that," said Dan.

"Now you do," Mel said. "I'm getting hungry."

"Okay."

"Are we speaking with Janet today?" Red asked.

"It's getting late," Dan replied. "We'll go see her tomorrow after my meeting."

"Your meeting?" Red asked. "After your meeting we'll only have about twenty-nine hours till Marrone puts bullets in all our heads. Is the meeting really that important?"

"Yes, it is," Dan replied. "And what the hell was all that about the policy being doubled if her death had something to do with acting?"

"I thought it was a good story," Red replied.

"Yeah, it's a good story, but only if you're not the one who has to come up with the money."

"You weren't really forking over that dough, were ya?"

"We gotta give the poor guy something, and now, thanks to you, we gotta give him double."

"How much were you gonna give him?"

"I was thinking five grand."

"So then double would be ten grand."

"Wow! Did that in your head, did ya? You're a regular *mathe-magician*."

# Chapter Thirty-Two

Monday morning Dan sat in the exact same spot in the Big Pine Methodist Church that he had for the last month and a half. The brunette he only knew as Ava sat in her same seat. Lance Beacon's seat was empty. Hal, the moderator, asked if anyone else had anything to share. No one did, so he excused the group and said, "See ya next week, people. One day at a time."

When Ava got up, she turned, and smiled at Dan. Dan smiled back. He let her exit her row of chairs first and walk down the aisle.

As Dan put his hand on his door handle he heard someone say, "Rick?"

Dan turned. It was Ava.

"I, um … I'm not usually this forward," Ava said. "But I was wondering if you would like to get a cup of coffee. There's a bagel shop in the mall across the street and …"

Dan thought about Maxine. He knew this was just coffee, but he also hoped Maxine wasn't having coffee with some guy either, or anything else for that matter.

"I really can't, Ava," said Dan. "I have an appointment at noon, and I'm probably gonna be late as it is."

"I understand."

"Maybe another time."

"Sure."

Ava turned and went toward her car. Dan watched her butt as she crossed the parking lot. He was pissed that Maxine wasn't here.

Just then, Beacon's Subaru with the shattered back window entered the parking lot. He came to a stop and jumped out of the car. "Hey, Coast!"

Dan quickly looked around the area to make sure no one heard Beacon use his real name. "Hey, Lance," he said.

"I thought I might miss you."

"Ya didn't."

"Meeting over?"

"Yup." Dan turned his head and watched Ava's car as it exited the parking lot.

Beacon pulled his check book out of his back pocket. "I'm on my way back home and I thought I would stop by and pay you. What do I owe ya?"

"I don't take checks," Dan said.

"I've only got a couple hundred bucks on me."

"You can owe me."

"Really?"

"Yeah. Something tells me you and I will see each other again someday."

Beacon looked confused. "Why do you say that?"

"You're bound to do something stupid again."

"Ha-ha. You're probably right. I better get going." Beacon stuck out his hand and Dan shook it.

"Make sure you find a meeting to go to up there in Cutler Bay."

"Naw," Beacon said. "I think I'm cured." He turned and climbed back into his car.

"Yeah, I bet you are," Dan said. "Like I said, I'll see you again some time."

Beacon pulled out of the parking lot and Dan climbed into his car. He took out his cell phone and dialed Red.

"Hello?" Red said.

"I'm leaving the meeting now. You ready to go."

"I'll be ready when you get here. Just hurry up."

"You nervous about dying?"

"I've been Googling how to fake my own death all morning."

"Ha! You don't have enough money for that."

"No, but you do."

"But like I said, you don't."

"Thanks a lot."

"What are friends for?" Dan put the Porsche in drive and headed for Key West.

# Chapter Thirty-Three

"Wow," Red commented, when they pulled up in front of the large two-story brick home at 3726 Sunrise Lane. "I guess Cousin Janet did do okay for herself."

"Looks that way," Dan concurred. He pulled the Porsche into the stone horseshoe-shaped driveway and shut off the engine. "Let's go see why she wanted Maria to play a trick on our missing boy and his brother."

"Should we call Joey?" Red asked.

"Let's see where this goes first."

Dan and Red walked to the front door and Dan gave the brass knocker a few swings, and then pushed the doorbell button. A loud gong of a bell rang out from somewhere inside.

"You rang?" Red said in his best Lurch imitation.

"What knockers," said Dan

"Sank you, Doctor."

The door opened. "May I help you?" asked a woman in her late fifties. She had gray hair pulled back in a short ponytail, and wore a classic maid uniform—black dress with a white, frilly apron and matching collar.

Dan reached for his business card and offered it. "I'm Dan Coast, and this Is Red Baxter. We're investigators working for the Waterfront Theater. We're wondering if we could ask Mrs. Troxler a few questions regarding the death of her cousin, Maria."

The woman snatched the card from Dan's fingertips. "Wait here, please," she said, and shut the door.

"That Mel Brooks was funnier than shit," Red said.

"What do you mean, was?" Dan asked.

"I think he's dead."

"I don't think he is."

"Maybe I'm thinking of Leslie Nielsen."

"Surely you can't be thinking of Leslie Nielsen."

"Stop calling me—"

The door opened again. "Please come in," said the maid.

Dan and Red entered into a large foyer with a marble floor and a fifteen foot ceiling.

"Mrs. Troxler will receive you in the parlor." The woman turned; they followed her to a doorway that opened into a huge living room.

Janet sat on the sofa dressed in pink silk pajama bottoms and a matching top. Her jet-black hair and makeup looked as though it had been professionally done only moments before Dan and Red's arrival.

"You'll have to excuse me," Janet apologized. "I'm not usually still in my evening wear at this late hour of the morning."

A silver tray sat on a coffee table in front of her. On the silver tray was a crystal pitcher filled with orange juice and a silver ice bucket. Four matching glasses surrounded the pitcher.

"And you'll have to excuse us for dropping by unannounced," Dan said.

"Please have a seat," Janet said, gesturing toward the chairs across from her.

"Thank you," said Dan.

"Would you care for a mimosa?" Janet asked. "I was just going to pour one for myself."

"No, thank you," said Dan.

"Yes, please," Red replied.

Janet poured a drink for Red and then one for herself.

"Thank you," Red said, and returned to his seat.

"I'm glad you didn't make me drink alone," Janet said. "They say you have a problem if you drink alone."

"Yeah," Dan responded, "but who are they, and what do they know?"

"Exactly," Janet agreed.

"It's five o'clock somewhere," Red added.

Janet chuckled. "He's cute," she said, pointing at Red.

"Cuter than a bug's ear," Dan agreed.

"So, what can I do for you gentlemen?" Janet asked.

"Maria had a small life insurance policy through the theater company," Dan began. "And we're working with the Waterfront Theater to determine if her death was theater related."

The smile left Janet's face. "I didn't realize the theater offered something like that."

"Yes," Dan continued. "We spoke with Maria's husband, Jack, yesterday, and he informed us that Maria was coming from your house when she was struck and killed."

"He did, did he?"

"Yes and he also said you had hired her for an acting job."

"I … well, it wasn't a real acting job. It was just—"

"Just what, Mrs. Troxler? Did you hire her for an acting gig?"

"It was nothing to do with the theater."

"What was it to do with?"

"You know, gentlemen, I just remembered I have an appointment. I must excuse myself. Show yourselves out please."

"Mrs. Troxler, who were the two men your husband wanted Maria to act for?"

"Please leave."

"Would you rather speak with the cops, Mrs. Troxler?"

Janet went for the phone. "I think maybe I'll call the cops. My husband is a very important man on this island."

"Isn't everyone?" Dan said. He and Red got up and went for the door.

"She's obviously hiding something," Red pointed out, as they drove back down Sunrise Lane.

"I'll call Joey after I drop you off and give him all the information we have. See where he wants to go from there."

"Maybe he can talk Eli Marrone into not shooting us." Red pointed at the clock on the dashboard. "We've only got about twenty-six hours to live."

"Maybe I should get you to a hospital," said Dan in a monotone

Red grinned. "A hospital? What is it?"

"It's a big building with patients. But that's not important right now."

Both men laughed uproariously.

"Feel better now?" said Dan.

"Yeah. Thanks, pal. I can always count on you."

# Chapter Thirty-Four

"Six hours," Red said.

"Shut up," Dan replied. He drove along A1A, headed toward Miami.

"You got a plan?"

"A plan for what?" Dan asked.

"A plan for when our time is up."

"Cremation, I guess."

"Very funny," said Red. He gazed out over the ocean as they drove along. "So you called Joey yesterday and he just told us to come up to Miami?"

"I called him after I dropped you off at your place. I gave him all the information we had. Then, about three hours later, he called me back and said for us to meet him at McSwain's office at two."

"By the time we get up there, we'll only have a little over two hours left. Our time will be up by the time we get back to Key West."

"You're really focused on that clock aren't ya?"

"Do you think we should give Eli Marrone a call?"

"Christ no," Dan replied. "I don't ever want to speak to him or see him again."

"So, you are nervous."

"Of course I'm nervous, but I don't want to talk about it."

Fine, we'll talk about something else. What did you do with Mel this morning?"

"Bev came over to stay with him."

"How's that new dog working out? What's his name, Boozer?"

"He's a pain in this ass. Buddy has barely come home the whole time that dog's been there."

"What are ya gonna do with it after Mel leaves?"

"I have no idea. Put an ad in the paper, I guess."

"You can't do that. Mel would be devastated."

"Well, I don't want two goddamn dogs. One is bad enough."

"Quit with the angry tough guy act. Everyone knows you love that dog of yours."

"Yeah, he's great."

"Maxine called lately?"

"Not since last Tuesday."

"She's gonna be sad after Marrone kills you."

"What the Christ!"

"Sorry!"

# Chapter Thirty-Five

Dan parked in the same parking garage he parked in the last time he and Red visited the McSwain and Cardiff Law Firm. This time, however, Dan pulled into the first spot he found, instead of driving all the way up to the roof. The two men didn't speak as they exited the garage and made their way across North Bayshore Drive to the entrance of the building at 555 North East Fifteenth Street.

This time, when they stepped off the elevator, the receptionist smiled and said, "They're waiting for you in Mr. McSwain's office, Mr. Coast."

"Thank you," Dan said.

The receptionist watched Red cross the room and winked when he caught her looking.

Red jabbed Dan in the ribs. "Did ya see that?" he asked.

"See what?'

"The receptionist, she winked at me."

"You're a beautiful man," said Dan.

"Well, yeah, I know it, but she's the third woman who flirted with me since I found out I was going to die."

"Huh. Maybe it's like being married."

"What do you mean?"

"They say married guys get hit on more than single guys. Maybe you're more attractive to women when you're about to die."

"That's just great."

Dan turned the knob and pulled open the door to McSwain's office, and they went inside.

McSwain sat behind his desk. Joey P sat in the same spot on the sofa as the last time. Tony Bianchi stood sentinel next to Joey. The only difference was, this time Eli Maronne sat at the other end of the sofa, and three of his men were stationed around the room.

"Oh, shit," Red whispered to himself. "This is it."

One of Marrone's goons pushed the door shut and stepped behind them. He frisked Red first and then Dan. When he lifted the back of Dan's T-shirt he found the 9mm and removed it. The muscle-bound bodyguard walked over and handed the weapon to Marrone.

Dan shrugged his shoulders. "You can never be too careful," he announced. "Miami can be a dangerous city."

Joey eyed the pistol. "My brother's gun," he said, and smiled. Joey was still under the impression that his brother Jimmy had given the weapon to Dan as a gift. Only Dan and Red knew the real story of how Dan stole the gun, and then used it to kill Jimmy.

Marrone handed Joey the gun.

"Sit down, guys," Joey said. "Take a load off."

Dan and Red took seats in the chairs across from McSwain. Marrone and Joey were to their right.

Dan looked around the room; no one was speaking. "So," he said, "does everyone know where we stand on this whole money/nephew missing thing?"

"I've passed the information you gave me along to Mr. Marrone," said Joey. "But I wanted to wait until you got here to fill in Mr. McSwain."

McSwain looked a little surprised. "Information?" he asked. "I wasn't aware there was … any information."

"Yes," Joey explained. "Dan seems to have uncovered something."

"Uncovered?" asked McSwain.

Dan was a little surprised as well. He wasn't quite sure what he had uncovered.

"Tell McSwain what you've learned so far, Dan," said Joey.

"Well, we found out that the woman who lured Ricky out of the Wounded Parrot was an actress."

"An actress, McSwain," Joey repeated. "Can you imagine that?"

"Really?" said McSwain.

"And tell him what happened to the actress, Dan."

Dan scanned the room. "She was run over and killed on her way home from her cousin's house."

"Her cousin who hired her to lure Ricky out of the bar," Joey added. "Isn't that right, Dan?"

"Yes it is," Dan replied.

McSwain's eyes went from Joey, to Marrone, and back to Dan. A bead of sweat was forming on his forehead. Dan noticed a color change in McSwain's face. He recalled what Jack Blair had told him. *Janet's brother in-law is an attorney up in Miami*, he thought. *Christ!*

"What did you say the actress's last name was, Dan?" Joey asked.

"Blair."

"Blair," said Joey. "There was something about that name. When Dan told me, I thought: I know I've heard that name before. But it was the next name he gave me, that's when it came to me." Joey stood and faced Dan. "Tell McSwain the cousin's name."

"Troxler."

Joey raised and shook his index finger. "There it is. Troxler. Now, McSwain, I know *you've* heard that name before."

McSwain said nothing. A drop of sweat ran down his cheek and landed on his day planner.

"McSwain, wasn't your father's name Troxler?" Joey asked. "And your stepbrother—your stepmother's son—isn't his name Troxler?"

McSwain put up his hand. "Mr. Pantucco, I can explain."

"Can you?" Joey asked. His eyes were focused on McSwain like a hawk on a field mouse.

"Everything I had was invested with my brother," McSwain explained. "He made some bad moves and—"

"Were any of them as bad as the move you've made?" Joey asked.

Red and Dan watched as the scene unfolded; neither spoke.

"Where's my nephew, McSwain?"

"He's dead," McSwain whispered. "He tried to fight back and—"

"You motherfucker!" Tony shouted, and moved toward McSwain.

Joey put up his hand, halting Tony.

"Where's my money?" Marrone asked.

"At my brother's house," McSwain answered.

Still facing Dan, and not even looking at McSwain, Joey Pantucco reached inside his sport coat and pulled a chrome 9mm semi-automatic pistol from his shoulder holster. The weapon was an exact duplicate of the one Dan had gotten from Joey's brother Jimmy, except a silencer was screwed to the end of Joey's barrel. Dan wondered if Joey had received his gun from his father on his eighteenth birthday, just as his brother Jimmy had.

McSwain's eyes doubled in size when he saw the 9mm. He started to speak, but the barrel flashed, and at that exact same moment a small red blossom appeared on McSwain's forehead. His head snapped back and blood and brain spattered the window behind him. His head dropped on the desk.

Dan jumped up. "Jesus Christ!" he said. He stared at the blood stain, and then through it at the sailboats in the harbor.

Joey returned his weapon to the holster and strolled over to the door. He pushed it open just a crack. "Ms. Jones, can you have Mr. Cardiff come in here, please?" he asked the receptionist. "And then tell the entire staff that everyone can go home early today. Mr. McSwain has a terrible headache."

"Yes, Mr. Pantucco," Ms. Jones replied.

Red stood slowly and turned to Dan. "So, then, we're gonna live, right?"

"I think so," answered Dan. He looked at Marrone questioningly.

"Yeah, you're off the hook, Coast. You and your fat friend."

Red winced at the insult. "Thank you for not killing us, Mr. Marrone, sir."

"Don't mention it."

Joey approached Dan and held out his hand.

"You want me to kiss your ring?" Dan quipped.

"Always the smart-ass, eh, Coast? No, I just wanted to thank you for all your hard work." He crunched a huge roll of cash into Dan's palm.

"Thanks, Joey."

"My pleasure, Coast." He gave Dan a playful sock on the chin. "Behave yourself … you and your fat friend."

"I'm not fat. I'm big boned," Red said under his breath, as they exited the office.

"Shut up," said Dan. "Just be glad you're alive."

Outside, Red asked Dan, "Can you give me Char's number?"

"I hope she still likes you—you know, now that you're not gonna die."

"Maybe I should tell her I have an incurable disease."

"You're a genius, pal."

"Thanks, buddy."

# Chapter Thirty-Six

"Come on, we gotta go, Mel," Dan said impatiently.

Mel sat in the floor of Dan's living room playing with Boozer. He would roll Buddy's tennis ball and bounce it off the wall. Boozer would run after it and bring it back to Mel.

"Good boy," Mel would say, each time. "I'm gonna miss Boozer."

"I know you will," Dan said. "I'll tell you what. Boozer can stay with me."

Mel turned and smiled at Dan. "I knew you liked him."

"No I don't."

"Yes you do, but he doesn't have to stay here. I have another idea."

Mel picked up the dog and Buddy's tennis ball and headed for the door. "Can you grab his water dish, Dan?" Mel asked.

"Sure."

Dan and Mel climbed into Dan's car and took off for the psych center. As they headed down Flagler Avenue, Mel pointed up ahead.

"Turn here," Mel said, as they approached Eighteenth Street.

Dan took a left and pulled to the curb in front of the Blairs' house. Both men climbed out of the car. Dan leaned against the fender with his arm folded in front of him. Mel walked up the steps to the door and knocked.

"Hi, Mel," Julia said, when she opened the door. She smiled when she saw Mel, and the smile grew when she saw the dog.

"Is your dad home?" Mel asked.

"Dad!" Julia shouted.

Jack Blair pulled the door open all the way. He looked past Mel at Dan and then back to Mel. "Yes?"

"Mr. Blair, I'm going away for a while," he explained, "and I need someone to look after my dog, Boozer." Mel set the dog down on the top step and Boozer rubbed his head against Julia's leg.

"Can we watch Boozer, Daddy?" Julia asked.

Blair watched his daughter as she played with the dog. "I think we can do that."

Mel handed Julia the tennis ball. "This is his best friend Buddy's tennis ball. He likes to play fetch." Mel proffered a plastic grocery bag. "I also brought his water dish and food bowl."

Julia threw her arms around Mel's legs. "Thank you, Mel. I'll take such good care of him."

"I knew you were the right person for the job."

"Everything is set with the insurance, Mr. Blair," Dan called out from the street. "You should be getting a check in the mail in the next few days."

"Thanks, Dan," said Blair.

Mel and Dan got back in the car and drove to the psych center.

"That was awful nice of you, Mel," Dan said.

Mel nodded his head and wiped a tear from his cheek. "I figured Julia could use a friend."

"Friends are important."

Mel turned to Dan. "We're friends—right, Dan?"

"You know it, pal,"

Mel leaned forward and pushed the power button on the radio. "I think this calls for a little electronic dance music."

"Boy, does it," said Dan.

# Chapter Thirty-Seven

The sun was just setting as Dan rounded the corner onto Beach View Street. He had taken the long way home and stopped at the Key West Cigar Club to pick up just the right cigar for a tequila, Seven, and lime by the fire pit. He chose a six-inch Camacho with a Maduro wrapper. He couldn't wait to get home and lit it in the car before his drive home.

Dan could see Maxine standing at the bottom of the steps as he approached his house. He felt a chill and the hair on his arms stood up. He pulled the Porsche into the driveway and shut off the engine.

"Hey," Maxine said.

"Hey," Dan replied. He got out of the car and took a long drag on the cigar.

"What's been going on?"

"Not much. Been kinda slow around here."

"What happened to the window?"

"Kids," Dan replied.

"I thought you would be at Red's. I was just about to drive over there."

Dan moved a little closer. "No. I figured I would stay in tonight. Maybe sit by the fire and have a smoke."

"Oh."

Dan took another step closer. "Are you back?" he asked.

Maxine nodded her head. "Yes."

Dan took another puff on his stogie. He removed it from his mouth and gently peeled off the wrapper. "I mean, to stay?" he asked.

Dan dropped the cigar on the sidewalk, took Maxine's hand in his, and got down on one knee. He held the cigar wrapper between his fingers and stared up at the woman he loved. "It's horrible when you're not here."

Maxine's eyes widened.

"Maxine Meyers, will you marry me?"

**The End**

**Coming Soon:**

**Sunrise City 3**
Never Strikes Twice

**We Call it Suicide**
A Dunquin Cove Story

## ALSO BY RODNEY RIESEL

**From the Tales of Dan Coast Series**

Sleeping Dogs Lie

Ocean Floors

The Coast of Christmas Past

Ship of Fools

Double Trouble

Most Likely to Die

Deadly Moves

On the Wagon

**Jake Stellar Series**

North Murder Beach

Beach Shoot

When Death Returns

The Obedience of Fools

Dead in the Water

**The Dunquin Cove Series**

The Man in Room Number Four

Return to Dunquin Cover

**Sunrise City Series**

Sunrise City

Sunrise City 2: From Bad to Worse

**Fernandina Beach Mysteries**

Maintenance Required

High Maintenance

**From Here to There:** A Collection of Short Stories

www.ingramcontent.com/pod-product-compliance
Lightning Source LLC
Chambersburg PA
CBHW071905220626

47052CB00002B/220